Trixie Belden #2

The Red Trailer Mystery

by Julie Campbell
illustrated by Mary Stevens
cover illustration by Michael Koelsch

Random House New York

www.randomhouse.com/kids

Library of Congress Cataloging-in-Publication Data
Campbell, Julie, 1908–1999.
[Trixie Belden and the red trailer mystery]
The red trailer mystery / by Julie Campbell ; illustrated by Mary Stevens ;
cover illustration by Michael Koelsch. — 1st Random House ed.
    p. cm. — (Trixie Belden ; #2)
SUMMARY: While traveling by trailer in upstate New York to find a runaway,
Trixie Belden and Honey Wheeler investigate a case of mysterious trailer
thefts.
ISBN 0-375-82411-1 (trade) — ISBN 0-375-92411-6 (lib. bdg.)
[1. Mystery and detective stories. 2. Trailers—Fiction.]
I. Stevens, Mary, ill. II. Koelsch, Michael, ill. III. Title. IV. Series.
PZ7.C1547 Re 2003 [Fic]—dc21 2002036951

Printed in the United States of America 10 9 8 7
First Random House Edition

RANDOM HOUSE and colophon are registered trademarks of Random House, Inc.

CONTENTS

Chapter 1
A Search Begins

Trixie saw her father's car turn into the driveway from Glen Road, and she raced out of the back door to stop him before he reached the garage.

"Dad! Dad!" she shouted. "We're going on a trailer trip, Honey Wheeler and I, with her governess, Miss Trask, to try and find Jim Frayne who has run away again."

Mr. Belden stopped the car by the steps leading to the back terrace. He leaned out of the window, smiling, but there was a puzzled frown on his face too. "What on earth are you talking about, Trixie? Who is Jim Frayne?"

Trixie put her arm on the car door. "He's old Mr. Frayne's great-nephew, Dad," she said, remembering that her parents hadn't guessed the secret of the mansion. "And now that Mr. Frayne is dead, Jim is his sole heir to a fortune of over half a million dollars. Isn't that wonderful?"

Mr. Belden nodded. "So they found the missing heir at last? When I left to drive your mother and Bobby to the seashore, they were still looking for the widow and her son."

"Jim's mother is dead, Dad," Trixie said. "And he ran away from his stepfather who beats him and makes him work on his farm for nothing. And Honey and I found him," Trixie went on excitedly, "and brought him food while he was hiding in the mansion, but now he's run away again. And, oh, Dad, I forgot to tell you, the old mansion burned to the ground last night."

Mr. Belden glanced up at the ruins on the eastern hill above the hollow. "I thought I smelled stale smoke when I turned into Glen Road," he said soberly. "That crumbling old house must have burned like tinder. It's a wonder, in the drought we've been having until the rain this morning, that the fire didn't spread through the woods to our place and the Wheeler estate."

"We were awfully afraid it would," Trixie told him as he got out of the car and walked with her to sit on the terrace. "And, Dad, this morning when Honey and I were up there, Mr. Rainsford arrived from New York. He's the executor of the estate, you know, and was looking for Jim because Mr. Frayne left all his money in trust for his nephew's son, who is Jim, you see. But Jim doesn't know that because he ran away early this morning. So now we've got to find him, Honey and I. That's why we're going on the trailer trip in the Wheelers' *Silver Swan,* which is really the darlingest little house on wheels you ever saw."

Trixie reached out and clutched her father's sleeve, begging, "Please, Dad, say I can go, *please!* Miss Trask, Honey's governess, is a wonderful driver and the best sport in the world. She has already phoned to Honey's parents in Canada for permission, and Mr. Rainsford is counting on our help."

Mr. Belden laughed and patted Trixie's brown hand. "It looks like it's pretty much settled, and I can't see any reason why I should object if Mr. and Mrs. Wheeler approve of the trip. But I don't quite see why a trailer trip is necessary. Couldn't Mr. Rainsford advertise in the papers for Jim and put detectives on his trail? It seems to me—"

"Oh, no, Dad," Trixie put in quickly, "that would ruin everything. Jonesy, Jim's stepfather, is his legal guardian, and Jim has made up his mind that he will never, never go back and live with him. Jonesy thinks Jim died in the fire last night—that's what the morning papers said—so now he has stopped looking for him. Jonesy doesn't care anything about Jim, Dad. He just wants to get control of the Frayne money. If anything appears in the papers about Jim being still alive, Jonesy will start looking for him again, and then Jim will run away and hide somewhere so we'll never find him."

"I'm beginning to understand something of what you're saying." Mr. Belden smiled. "But if Jim's stepfather is as cruel as you claim he is, why can't Mr. Rainsford take the matter to court and have another guardian appointed?"

"He's working on that now, Dad," Trixie said. "He's even got written proof from Jonesy's neighbors and everything, but the point is, we've got to find Jim first and tell him all that before Jonesy even guesses that Jim isn't dead."

Trixie hugged her knees rocking back and forth. "Oh, Dad, Jim is really the most wonderful boy I ever knew. His ambition in life is to own and run a camp for orphan boys so they can learn how to be good at sports and how to get along in the woods at the same time that they have school lessons. So that's why we feel sure he's trying now to get a job at one of those three big camps upstate. He could be a junior counselor, like Brian and Mart, or junior athletic instructor, because he's very good at everything, and although he's only fifteen, he did two years of high school in one, and won a scholarship to college—" Trixie stopped, completely out of breath.

"He sounds like a great lad," her father said, laughing. "But he's not going to have an easy time getting a job without written permission from his parents or guardian. I wrote several letters and had personal interviews with the operators of the camp where your brothers now have junior counselor jobs."

"I know," Trixie admitted. "And that's why we have to start right away to find him. He told Honey and me that if he didn't get a job at one of those three big camps, he'd ship aboard a cattle boat and go to Europe. And then we'd *never* find him."

"Well, then," Mr. Belden said mildly, "it seems to me that Mr. Rainsford should put detectives on the case immediately."

"Oh, don't you see, Dad?" Trixie moaned. "If Jim suspects detectives are trying to find him, he'll think for sure Jonesy hired them, and he'll leave the country right away. But if he hears that two girls are looking for him, he won't be worried at all because he trusts Honey and me. Please, Dad," she begged. "We want to start tomorrow early. Please say I may go!"

Mr. Belden stood up. "You have my permission, Trixie. How long do you plan to be gone?"

"Less than a week, Dad." Trixie followed her father into the house. "Shall I telephone Mother and see if she thinks it's all right?"

"I'll call her myself," Mr. Belden said. "As a matter of fact, this will work out very well. Your mother and Bobby planned to stay at the seashore until next weekend anyway, so it would be lonely here for you. I can get Mrs. Green out from the village to keep house for me."

As he picked up the phone with one hand he handed Trixie a crisp five-dollar bill with the other. "Here's your first week's salary," he grinned and, imitating Trixie, added, "Boy, oh boy, will you have a lot of weeding to do when you get back!"

"Thanks, Dad." Trixie laughed. "I'll go over every inch of the garden with eyebrow tweezers!"

"Well, a hoe anyway," her father returned. "Run along now and start packing if you want to leave early in the morning."

Trixie was yanking clothes out of her bureau drawers when her father called up the stair well that he had received her mother's approval of the plan. Leaving everything helter-skelter, she raced out of the house and up the hill to the Wheeler estate.

Trixie and her three brothers and their parents lived in a little white frame house down in the hollow, and the name of their place was Crabapple Farm. Recently the luxurious Manor House with its stables and lake and acres of rolling green lawn up on the western hill had been purchased by the Wheeler family from New York. Honey Wheeler and Trixie, who were both thirteen, had soon become fast friends.

"Honey! Honey!" Trixie shouted as she took the steps to the Manor House veranda two at a time. "Dad says I can. Oh, I can hardly wait!"

Honey and her governess were upstairs packing when Trixie burst into the dainty room with its white ruffled organdy curtains and matching bedspread. Miss Trask, an athletic-looking, middle-aged woman, pushed back a strand of her short gray hair and smiled at Trixie. "I'm so glad it's all settled," she said. "I was so sure your parents would approve that I sent Regan to the village for supplies. I want you girls to do most of the cooking on this trip. There's quite an efficient little kitchenette on the *Silver Swan,* and some of the trailer camps we may want to stop at along the way have water and electrical connections. I think it would be good for you and lots of fun to keep house while we're searching for Jim." ·

"Wonderful," Trixie cried enthusiastically. Actually, Trixie hated housework but cooking in a trailer sounded like camping out.

"I've always wanted to fool around in a kitchen,"

11

Honey said wistfully, "but none of our cooks would ever let me touch anything."

"Well," Miss Trask said briskly, "I think every girl, no matter what her position, should learn how to cook and keep house. And I also think that girls as well as boys should learn how to take care of themselves in the woods. I've packed a book with simple menus for both indoor and outdoor cooking. Some of the recipes sound delicious."

"I can cook," Trixie said proudly. "I fixed home-made baked beans for Dad's supper tonight. It's a cinch," she admitted with a grin. "You just put some pea beans into a pot with water, add chili sauce, garlic, onions, salt pork or bacon, and molasses, and bake the whole mess slowly for eight hours."

"Sounds divine," Honey said admiringly and added to Miss Trask, "When we find Jim he'll teach us how to take care of ourselves in the woods. He's a real woods-man and promised to show us how to skin and cook a rabbit on a spit and build a shanty tent between two trees, and—and everything!"

"I'm sorry you girls never gave me a chance to meet him," Miss Trask said. "Regan was telling us just now what a great lad Jim is and what an expert horseman."

"We wanted to tell you about him, Miss Trask,"

Honey said impulsively. "We knew we could trust you but we were pretty sure you'd feel he ought to go back to his guardian."

Honey, pushing back her bangs and tossing her shoulder-length, wavy, light-brown hair, turned to Trixie. Her huge hazel eyes were wide with sympathy for the runaway. "If it hadn't been for that awful Jonesy, we *would* have told Miss Trask about Jim, wouldn't we?"

Trixie nodded so vigorously that her sandy curls tumbled down on her tanned forehead. She was not quite as tall as Honey but a lot sturdier. Miss Trask glanced at her appraisingly.

"All of those sweaters, bathing suits, jerseys, and shorts that Honey wore at camp last summer are too small for her now," she told Trixie. "But they should fit you perfectly. Why don't you let me put the lot of them in this extra suitcase and bring them along? Then all you'd have to pack would be dungarees, underclothes, some socks, and an extra pair of shoes."

Trixie's round blue eyes sparkled at the sight of shelves stacked with expensive and almost new sports clothes. "Golly, that would be marvelous, Miss Trask," she breathed. "Most of my stuff is in rags. I simply can't sew," she admitted ruefully, "and Moms insists that I'm old enough to do my own mending."

"I'll do your mending, Trixie," Honey offered. "That's one thing that awful governess I had before you, Miss Trask, showed me how to do well." She laughed. "Mother can't sew or cook either and she doesn't approve of girls doing anything that might hurt their hands. She'd have a fit if she knew I'd been riding horses and bikes all week without gloves!"

It always made Trixie feel depressed to think about Honey's beautiful but spoiled mother so she quickly changed the subject.

"Well, I'd better go home now and fix Dad's supper," she said. "See you at the crack of dawn."

But they did not get off to an early start after all. At the last minute both girls decided to take their dogs, the Belden Irish setter, Reddy, and Honey's new cocker spaniel puppy, Bud.

And, of course, after they had packed everything inside the spacious chrome-trimmed sky-blue trailer, neither dog could be found. Finally Regan, the Wheelers' good-natured groom, located Bud, who had accidentally got shut into an empty horse stall. But although Trixie called and whistled for what seemed like hours, there was no sign of Reddy.

"We can't go off and leave him now," she wailed as it grew later and later. "Dad won't be home until suppertime and Mrs. Green isn't coming out from the village until five o'clock. Both of them will think Reddy is with us and so they won't even look for him. Something awful may have happened to him. I've *got* to find him!"

She and Honey tramped through the woods that ran between the Wheeler estate and the burned-down mansion, calling and whistling until noon. After lunch Trixie gave one last, discouraged shout, and this time there was an answering bark.

Reddy, minus his collar, his silky auburn coat matted with burrs, came bounding up from the hollow to the Wheeler driveway where the trailer was parked.

"Oh, Reddy," Trixie scolded him affectionately. "You've lost your collar again. You're just about the worst nuisance in the world!"

Regan reached down to pat the setter's head and said, "He's awfully hot and sweaty, Trixie. I think he must have got his collar caught in something and only just worked his way free." He straightened. "You can't take him without his license and identification tag. He might get lost on this trip. Can you remember his license number?"

Trixie told him what it was. "He's lost his collar so many times I know it by heart."

"Okay," Regan said. "I'll run into the village in the

station wagon and pick up another collar and have another tag made."

And so it was almost three o'clock when they finally set off on the Albany Post Road, driving north along the Hudson River.

At first Trixie and Honey rode in the trailer because Trixie had to examine carefully everything inside the house on wheels. Trixie was surprised that 200-odd square feet of floor space could hold so much. The back door, up one short step, opened into a combination living-room and bedroom with a cozy little dining alcove. Beyond that was a tiled kitchenette which Honey said her father referred to as the "galley." The glistening modern bathroom was equipped with a glassed-in shower, fluorescent lighting and a compact mirrored cabinet over the washbasin.

In the galley were an electric stove and refrigerator, and a stainless steel sink and worktable unit. The shelves and cabinets, which were covered with bright blue oil-cloth, were filled with all sorts of canned goods. The floor was covered with spotless blue and silver linoleum.

Wide-eyed, Trixie wandered back to the stern of the *Swan*. On one side was a convertible davenport where Miss Trask would sleep, Honey said, and on the other, trim double-decker bunks.

"I hicks the top bunk," Trixie cried, and then added, ashamedly, "unless you want it, Honey."

Honey was unpacking suitcases and stowing their contents on the shelves of compact cabinets built in behind sliding doors under the lower bunk. She looked up with a smile. "No, thanks. I'd be sure to get seasick or something." She pointed to a mirrored closet in one corner of the combination living-room and bedroom. "There are plenty of hangers if you want to put anything in there."

Trixie was still too stunned to unpack. "I never saw anything like this, Honey," she breathed. "It must have cost a mint!"

Honey shrugged. "I've seen much more luxurious ones, and Mother thinks this is so uncomfortable she won't travel in it. One of her friends has a coach that's thirty-eight feet long and has four rooms. It's air-conditioned, and I wish the *Swan* was. This is the hottest July I ever remember trying to live through!"

"It is hot," Trixie admitted, sinking down on the plaid-cushioned divan. "But it's not that I mind so much. It's the humidity—it's going to rain again before night, I'll bet."

After the girls had unpacked, Miss Trask stopped at a gas station, and then they joined her in the tow car, a gleaming midnight-blue sedan.

"I hope you don't mind this snail's pace," said Miss Trask from the front seat. "I'm a cautious driver to begin with and now I feel as though I were dragging an elephant behind us!"

At six o'clock she said over her shoulder, "A nice little trailer camp is shown on the map just this side of Poughkeepsie. Let's stop there for the night. We may not find another good place to park before dark, and I don't like the idea of driving around the countryside after dark."

"That reminds me," Honey said. "We haven't told Trixie about the camp where we're going to have our headquarters. It's in the farming district far upstate," she went on to Trixie, "and it's practically a little village, with a cafeteria that's really the clubhouse, and an outdoor movie, and not far away is a riding academy. I thought we might rent horses and ride to the three different camps Jim said he was interested in. The trailer village, which is called Autoville, is only a few miles from Pine Hollow Camp and Wilson Ranch and just a good long ride to that other boys' camp."

"Rushkill Farms, you mean," Trixie said. "That's the name of the third camp Jim mentioned. It'll be swell fun riding horseback to them. I'll drop Dad a post card as soon as we reach Autoville and give him the phone number in case he wants to get in touch with me."

"You can do it now," Honey said. "Miss Trask has already called the manager, who has offices in the cafeteria, to reserve parking space. When she telephoned Mother and Daddy yesterday, she gave them the number so they could have it in case—" She stopped and gazed out of the window at a glorious view of the Hudson River reflecting a purple and gold sunset.

Then they turned into a small trailer camp, and Trixie watched excitedly from the back seat while Miss Trask made arrangements with the owner for overnight space and electricity and water.

They parked beside another trailer, a big red one with *Robin* printed in small black letters on the door. Trixie stared at it, wondering why the shades on its windows were pulled down as though its occupants had already gone to sleep.

Then she yawned. "I'm starving."

"So am I," Miss Trask admitted. "Let's have supper and go right to bed like the people next door so we can get an early start tomorrow. We're way off schedule. I hoped we might spend this evening at Autoville, but what with the delay this morning and my over-cautious driving!" She chuckled. "I'm glad you girls are the chefs. I'm too tired to boil an egg."

They hurried inside the *Swan,* and Honey consulted the little cookbook. "We can frizzle a jar of chipped beef in a tablespoon of vegetable oil," she said, leading the way to the galley, "and add a can of mushroom soup to it and serve it with canned peas."

"Yummy-yum," Trixie shouted. "That sounds—" She stopped by the living-room window and gazed out with her mouth open. A man with shaggy black hair had just emerged from the trailer next door. He was wearing a threadbare suit and scuffed shoes, and the tight collar on his white shirt was frayed and worn.

"That's funny," Trixie wondered out loud. "What's such a man who looks so poverty-stricken doing in such a lavish trailer?"

Honey came out of the galley to peer over her shoulder. "Probably the chauffeur," she whispered. "But then why isn't he wearing a uniform like other chauffeurs?"

Bud and Reddy were scratching at the door, hinting that they had been cooped up inside the *Swan* too long. Trixie let them out, and they bounded in circles barking joyfully around the shaggy-haired man who, paying no attention to them, strode rapidly toward a nearby hot-dog stand. While the girls watched curiously from the entrance to the *Swan,* Bud and Reddy came back and began sniffing curiously around the entrance to the red trailer.

At that moment the *Robin*'s door opened a crack, and a little girl appeared. She was barefoot and her patched yellow sunsuit was faded and worn. Carefully she slipped her thin body through the crack in the doorway and tiptoed down the steps. Bud growled at her playfully and jumped up to lick her face.

"Nice puppy," she murmured, sitting down on the ground and gathering the little black cocker spaniel into her arms. "My nice puppy."

Honey laughed. "He's mine, but he likes you a lot."

"*Mine,*" the little girl insisted, frowning. "All black puppies belong to me!"

Trixie giggled and whispered, "She sounds just like my brother Bobby and I guess she is just about his age. Don't you think so?"

Honey nodded. "She's cute," and added under her breath, "but she looks half-starved. If her parents are rich enough to own a big trailer like that, you'd think they'd feed her decently and dress her in something better than rags!"

"It's not polite to whisker," the little girl said, staring at them disapprovingly. "Only naughty people whisker. My name's Sally. What's yours?"

Before Trixie or Honey could reply, the door to the red trailer was suddenly thrown open, and a tired-faced woman came out on the top step. Her cheap cotton house dress was neat and clean but it showed signs of too frequent washing and mending. She was holding a tiny sick-looking baby in her thin arms and another child, in threadbare overalls, crawled behind her to peer out with big, expressionless eyes.

"Sally," the woman called shrilly. "Come back inside at once!"

Sally promptly burst into tears, rubbing her blue eyes with grimy fists. "I won't, I won't. I'm sick n' tired of staying indoors all the time."

Her mother, completely ignoring Trixie and Honey, came quickly down the steps. She seized the little girl's shoulder and shook her gently. "You're naughty, *very* naughty. You know you're not supposed to speak to strangers."

Sally squirmed away from her and picked up Bud in her thin little arms. "I'll come back if you let me take my puppy with me."

The woman gasped and turned a shade paler, her lips almost white. As Honey said afterward, she looked as shocked as though the child had said something really dreadful.

Impulsively, kindhearted Honey called, "It's all right. He's my dog but she can play with him inside the trailer for as long as she likes."

Sally's mother caught her lower lip between her teeth and there were tears in her eyes, but she replied coldly, "I'll not allow any such a thing! The idea of her saying it is her dog." She raised her voice. "Joeanne, *Joeanne!*"

A slim, eleven-year-old girl with black pigtails hurried out of the trailer. She was wearing faded blue jeans and a shirt that was so much too small for her that Honey and Trixie could plainly see her protruding shoulder blades as she bent over and scooped Sally into her arms, puppy and all.

"Never mind, darling," they heard her croon as Bud broke away and ran to Honey. "You'll have another puppy some day. One all your own."

"I want him," Sally wailed, hiding her teary face in her sister's neck. "He's *mine.*"

And then the shaggy-haired man came hurrying back from the hot-dog stand with a paper plate of sandwiches and a quart of milk in a container. He was frowning darkly as he set the food inside the trailer and reached out a long, muscular arm to snatch Sally away from her sister.

"Get inside, all of you," he muttered in a harsh, bitter undertone. "Quick!"

The tired-faced woman cringed as though she had been slapped, and she meekly obeyed, taking the two babies with her. But Joeanne stood defiantly for a moment, staring at her father as though she had never seen him before, and as they glared at each other Trixie thought she had never seen two people who looked more alike.

Both of them were deeply tanned with taut, wiry muscles, and, Trixie reflected with an inward laugh, if the father didn't do something about his shaggy black hair soon, he would have to braid it into two pigtails to keep it out of his eyes.

"I'm sorry about all this," Joeanne was saying quietly over her shoulder to Trixie and Honey. "My little sister doesn't understand. We had a black cocker puppy once but he died." Then with a toss of her long black braids she marched stiffly inside the *Robin* behind her father and slammed the door.

One of the babies began to cry, but there was no other sound inside the red trailer. No one spoke, at least not loud enough for Trixie or Honey to hear what he or she said.

Chapter 2
Sobs in the Night

Honey stared at Trixie. "Did you ever hear of such a peculiar family? There they are all inside that trailer and no one is speaking to anybody else. I hope they give that baby some milk soon. It sounds as though it were starving."

"They all looked starved," Trixie said. "And yet they must have plenty of money if they own that big red trailer. I caught a glimpse of the inside just before Joeanne closed the door and it looks as though it must have cost almost as much as the *Swan* did. It has double-decker bunks made of maple and newly painted shelves and shiny floors and everything." She stopped, frowning thoughtfully. "You know, Honey, I think I've been inside that trailer sometime or other, but I can't remember when or where."

"You may have seen pictures of it in some magazine," Honey suggested. "Ours has been written up lots of times along with ones owned by movie stars. As a matter of fact," she finished, "the *Swan* originally belonged to a movie star who got bored with it and sold it to Dad. He bought it for Mother's birthday last year but she doesn't like it."

But Trixie wasn't listening. She was thinking about the shaggy-haired man and his hungry family. "Do you suppose that man is a mean old miser?" she asked Honey. "Like Jim's great-uncle was? Old Mr. Frayne used to go around looking like a scarecrow and he never had enough to eat."

"I don't know what to think," Honey admitted. "I liked that girl with the pigtails—Joeanne. She was the only one who didn't act afraid of her father."

"Oh, look," Trixie cried. "She dropped one of her hair ribbons." She stooped and picked up the faded bow of frayed blue sateen. "I'm going to take it back to her. It'll give me a good excuse to see inside the *Robin.* Then maybe I'll remember where I saw it before."

"You've got more nerve than I have," said Honey, giggling nervously. "I'm scared of that long-haired man. He looks mean enough to bite."

Trixie ignored her and hurried across the space between the two trailers. She rapped on the door and it was opened immediately by Joeanne herself. "You dropped this," Trixie began, but the little girl quickly took the ribbon and closed the door again before Trixie could say another word.

"Well," Trixie said as she joined Honey on the *Swan* steps, "I got another glimpse, and you know what? They were sitting on the bunks, staring into space, except for the father and he was holding his head in his hands."

Honey laughed. "Now don't tell me that wailing baby was sitting on a bunk. It's too young for one thing and probably much too weak from hunger to do anything but cry."

Trixie flushed with impatience. "I meant the mother and the other two children. Sally was sort of sulking but the little boy in overalls was just sitting there with the most awful vacant look in his face. It made me feel as though they had all given up hope, as if they didn't care much what happened to them." She shuddered. "It's all so mysterious. Why aren't they supposed to speak to strangers? Why did the mother look so shocked when Sally said Bud was her puppy?"

"And why," Honey finished, "do they keep the shades down on a hot evening like this when they haven't even gone to bed?"

Miss Trask came to the door of the *Swan* then. "I thought you two girls were going to fix a delicious meal." She handed them each an apron. "We must eat and go right to bed so we can get an early start tomorrow. We wasted half a day this morning looking for Reddy."

"I know," Honey said as she and Trixie got to work

28

with a can opener and a frying pan. "We told Dad we'd arrive at Autoville tomorrow at the latest so we've got to in case he or Mother call to see if we arrived safely."

Trixie stirred the dried beef in the hot oil, then added the thick, creamy mushroom soup while Honey buttered the toast and cut it into little squares.

"Let's save on dish-washing," Trixie said with a grin. She hated indoor work and always did her chores at home just as fast as she could. "If I add a can of peas to this goulash, there'll be one less pan to wash."

Miss Trask laughed good-naturedly. "All right this once. But no more short cuts. I want three-course meals from now on."

The dinner was delicious although it took only a few minutes to prepare, and Trixie ate so much she fell asleep almost the minute she climbed into her bunk. The top deck she had chosen was on the side next to the red trailer. It began to rain in the night, at first a gentle patter, but after a while it came down in an angry torrent.

Trixie awoke with a start when the cold rain splashed in her face and she hastily closed the window beside her bunk. Honey had already closed the other windows with Miss Trask's help.

"You certainly sleep soundly," Honey said. "We have been shouting at you to wake up for a long time."

Trixie swung her legs over the side of her bunk and

grinned down at them. "Isn't this cozy? I love being all snug and warm inside and listening to the sound of rain coming down on the roof."

"I do too," Miss Trask said, "but this is a little too snug and warm for me. It's going to get awfully stuffy in here if we can't open the windows soon."

"Mother can't stand the Hudson River Valley in July and August," Honey said. "She says it's not only the heat but the humidity! That's why Dad took her on a trip to Canada."

The rain continued and the windows inside the trailer became clouded with steam. Trixie curled up on top of her bed and tried to go to sleep. *Poor Honey,* she thought, *she can't help thinking about her mother and wondering why she doesn't behave like other mothers.*

Honey had admitted to Trixie the very first day they met that she hardly knew her parents and had been brought up by nurses and governesses between boarding school and camp. Honey was, indeed, a poor little rich girl, and Trixie hoped that when the Canadian trip was over Honey and her mother would turn over a new leaf and try to get to know each other. Trixie could not bear to see anyone unhappy and she knew that although Honey loved Miss Trask, she craved the kind of mother Trixie herself had.

"But still," Trixie told herself, "she's not as bad off as Jim who's an orphan. We've *got* to find him and then maybe, as Honey hopes, the Wheelers will adopt him so she can have a brother. He'll like Brian and Mart and we can all go to school together next fall and have such good times in the winter, skiing and sledding and skating."

Having Jim as a neighbor was such a pleasant thought that Trixie began to dream about the fun they could all have if things worked out right, and while she dreamed, the rain faded into a drizzle and finally stopped altogether.

Sleepily Trixie raised the window beside her bunk and went back to her dreams. Suddenly her happy thoughts were rudely interrupted by very unhappy sounds from the next trailer. A woman was weeping softly as though she could no longer keep her misery bottled up inside her.

And then a man's voice, harsh and argumentative, rose above the quiet sobs. Trixie could only hear snatches, but what she heard jarred her into wide-awakeness.

"It's got to be this way, I tell you. It's the only way out—"

And then the woman. "Oh, no, Darney. It's wrong. We should have known better. Look at what it's doing already to Sally and Joeanne. I can't bear it. I can't bear it. You've got to take it back at once. It may already be too late."

Trixie's heart ached for the sobbing woman, and she pulled the sheet over her head to shut out the sound of the voices in the *Robin*. But the man was hoarsely whispering, "Don't be an idiot. We've got to go ahead with it. No one will ever know. And as for Joeanne and Sally, you should have let me—"

"Sh-h," the woman cautioned. "You'll awaken them. Go to sleep now, Darney. We'll talk about it again in the morning."

"A fine thing," the man grumbled. "My own family turning against me! You were all for it in the beginning, Sarah."

"I know, I know," the woman moaned. "But I didn't realize then—"

Whatever she was going to say was lost in muffled sobs. Then there was silence. A silence that made Trixie remember how, earlier, the family had sat together, staring vacantly into space.

"What is the matter with that family?" she wondered, tossing and turning in the hot, humid air. "Why do they all act as though they don't care what happens to them? What is it the mother thinks should be taken back before it's too late?"

Still wondering, Trixie dropped off to sleep but again, much later, she was awakened by sounds from the other trailer. At first she thought she was still dreaming, but then, gradually, she realized with bewilderment that this time it was a *man* who was sobbing. His breath was coming and going in the choked gasps of someone whose spirit is broken!

Trixie sat up, and in spite of the heat, she felt little goose pimples of horror icily prickling her bare arms.

Surely it couldn't be the harsh-voiced, shaggy-haired man who was weeping! Then it must be someone else. Was it a helpless person who was being held against his will in the red trailer?

Was he the something who should be returned before it was too late?

Trixie, listening to the deep, regular breathing that was coming from the other bunks in the *Swan* felt lonely and frightened. Should she wake Miss Trask and tell her that someone in the next trailer needed help? If the man who was sobbing in those dry-throated gasps had been kidnaped, the police should be notified at once.

And then the sounds ceased as though whoever it was had buried his face in a pillow—or, Trixie couldn't help wondering—had suddenly been smothered into silence.

Chapter 3
A Rescue

In spite of herself, Trixie fell into an exhausted sleep, still wondering about the mysterious occupants of the red trailer parked alongside the *Swan*. When she awoke the sun was streaming through the rain-washed windows and Miss Trask was already dressed.

"The dogs woke me at dawn," she said. "I let them out for a run. We may as well have breakfast at the hot-dog stand. It'll save time."

Honey was sleepily buttoning the front of her thin cotton shirt the tail of which she had tucked inside her seersucker shorts. "It's too hot for a jersey and slacks," she told Trixie. "I advise you to wear the coolest things you can find, and let's open all the windows. It's stifling in here."

Trixie slipped into a white playsuit and helped Miss Trask open the windows they had closed during the rain in the night. Then they shut the dogs inside the trailer.

"One good thing about Reddy," Trixie said as they hurried over to the hot-dog stand, "is that he won't try to jump through those screens and follow us. But he did go right through a window once. Remember, Honey?"

Honey nodded. "I don't think either of them will try to leave the trailer till we get back. At least I hope not. They've caused enough delays as it is."

Honey sounded so hot and cross and Miss Trask seemed to be in such a hurry to get started that Trixie decided not to tell them about the sobbing she had heard from the next trailer until later. As she drank her orange juice and ate her cereal, everything seemed so peaceful and quiet in the trailer camp that Trixie began to wonder if perhaps she had dreamed the mysterious conversation she had half listened to the night before.

When they came out of the hot-dog stand, she saw at once that the red trailer, which only a few minutes ago had been parked beside the *Swan,* was gone. And bounding across the mud puddles in the rutted road was Reddy, joyfully barking a greeting.

"Now how did he get out of the trailer?" Honey demanded. "Honestly, Trixie, that dog is more trouble than a dozen puppies."

Trixie laughed good-naturedly. "He's nothing but an overgrown puppy, I guess. I sure hope he didn't go through a screen. The mosquitoes will eat us alive tonight if he did."

Miss Trask frowned as they hurried across the road to the *Swan*. "I locked the door," she said, "and it's still locked. Oh, dear, look. One of the screens has been raised. We must have overlooked it when we opened the windows, Trixie."

Trixie stared at the low, screenless window. "I could have sworn they were all shut," she said thoughtfully. "And they must have been. None of us has had any reason to raise a screen since we started on the trip, and Regan checked them all before we left."

"That's right," Honey said. "I checked them all myself because one single buzzing mosquito can keep me awake all night." She followed Miss Trask inside the trailer with Trixie right behind her. "Oh, dear," she admitted after a quick look around, "Now I'm not sure that either Regan or I *did* check that little window. We hardly ever open it because it's so small and it's so low it just lets in a lot of dust without cooling off the place enough to make it worth while. Wouldn't you know," she finished impatiently, "that Reddy would smell out the one open window?"

Trixie grinned. "How about Buddy? I don't see any sign of *your* pup, Honey!"

Honey's eyes widened. "Why, that's true! Now where can he be?"

She began to whistle and call, but there was no answering bark from the little black cocker spaniel.

"Oh, dear," Miss Trask complained. "It was a mistake taking those dogs with us. Another early start ruined!"

Honey looked as though she were going to cry. "I know something awful has happened to him! He might have got run over by one of those big heavy trailers that left while we were having breakfast."

"Don't even think of such a thing," Trixie said with quick sympathy. "He's probably playing with some little boy or girl in the camp. You know how he loves children and how they love him, Honey."

But a door-to-door questioning of all their neighbors proved fruitless. Nobody had seen the black puppy. At ten o'clock even Honey gave up.

"He may have wandered off into the woods," Miss Trask said finally, glancing at her wrist watch. "If so, he'll come back when he gets hungry. I'll leave the Autoville phone number with the proprietor of this camp so he can call us when Buddy does turn up."

Honey was trying hard to keep back the tears. "Let's tack up a reward notice in the cafeteria," she said. "Then if anyone finds him they'll be sure to let us know."

Trixie, who had been staring down at the mud in

front of the *Swan,* said, "Look at these footprints! They're too small to be Reddy's and they go back and forth between here and where the red trailer was parked." She straightened. "You know what I think? I think Buddy got confused when the *Robin* left camp. He may have followed the red trailer thinking we were in it and had gone off and left him. Puppies often do that sort of thing, Honey, and Buddy had hardly had time yet to realize that the *Swan* is his home."

Honey immediately brightened. "Then maybe we'll find him somewhere along the Post Road?"

"That's right," Trixie said comfortingly.

Miss Trask came back then from talking with the proprietor in the hot-dog stand, and in a few minutes the *Swan* was on its way again. Trixie and Honey kept their eyes glued to the road, hoping for some sign of the little black puppy. By noon Honey had given up all hope.

"He's too little to have traveled this far," she said mournfully. "Oh, Trixie, I know we'll never see him again."

"Oh, yes, we will," Trixie said firmly. "You never had a dog before so you don't understand them. If Bud found he couldn't keep up with the *Robin,* he probably turned around and went back to the trailer camp. He may even have gone all the way back home. Dogs are awfully smart about directions, you know."

Honey blinked back her tears. "You mean like the dog in *Lassie Come Home?*"

Trixie nodded briskly. "That's one of my favorite books. Do you remember, the collie traveled a thousand miles to get back to her master?"

"You're right, Trixie," Miss Trask said. "When we arrive at Autoville we'll put through a call to Regan at once. And now let's decide where we want to have lunch. There's a picnic ground beside a lake not far from here. Wouldn't you girls like to take a swim and cool off before we eat?"

Honey, in spite of her worries about Buddy, enthusiastically agreed to this plan. At the next intersection Miss Trask drove off to the right and up a wooded hill to the public picnic grounds. She parked beside a rustic table flanked by two weather-beaten benches and pointed to a nearby outdoor oven.

"I'll roast potatoes while you're swimming," she said. "Then you can broil those hamburgers I bought at the hot-dog stand, and toast marshmallows for dessert."

"Wonderful," Honey cried, cheering up at the thought.

But Trixie wasn't listening. She was staring across the lake shading her blue eyes from the sun. "Do you see what I see?" she said in a low voice to Honey. "Isn't that a red trailer over there parked under the trees? Doesn't it look like the *Robin* to you?"

Honey squinted in the direction Trixie was pointing. "Why yes," she said after a moment. "I'm sure it's the *Robin!* Oh, Trixie, maybe they discovered Buddy was following them and picked him up. Let's go right over and ask them."

Miss Trask had disappeared into the woods to gather kindling so the girls called out, "We'll be right back," and started along the path that wound around the lake.

As they hurried toward the other shore, Trixie told Honey about the mysterious conversation she had overheard the night before.

"And then," she finished, "there was the awful sound of a man crying, Honey. Do you think they could have kidnaped somebody?"

"It certainly sounds like it," Honey said and then stopped. "Look who's in wading. Isn't that Sally?"

The little girl saw them before Trixie could reply and immediately began to wave and splash her way across the lake in their direction.

"For a little girl who's not supposed to speak to strangers," Trixie giggled, "she certainly is friendly."

"I wish she'd stay closer to shore," Honey said nervously. "Lakes have a way of dropping off suddenly from a two-foot depth to—" She ended in a stifled scream as the child's head suddenly disappeared under the water as though her body had been sucked down by a deep-sea monster.

Trixie stood rooted to the spot with horror. Sally would certainly drown if they took the time to run around the lake to the shallow water where she had been wading. The child's head bobbed up and down again as the thin little arms helplessly flailed the water.

Trixie started for the lake. There was only one thing to do. They must try to swim across and save the child before it was too late.

But Honey, several yards ahead of Trixie, had already kicked off her moccasins and was tearing off her shirt as she ran through the water. Then, hitting the deep part of the lake, she began to swim with clean, fast strokes toward the little girl, holding the collar of her shirt in her mouth.

Trixie, knowing that Honey was a much better swimmer than she was, watched and waited, holding her breath. When Honey got near enough to those pathetic, flailing arms, she seized the collar of her shirt with one hand and threw the tail of it to Sally.

Sally grabbed and hung on. "Lie on your back and float," Honey ordered, and the little girl obeyed. It had all happened so quickly she had not had time to become badly frightened, so it was an easy matter for Honey to tow her into shallow water.

Trixie waded out to meet them and, waist deep, gathered the little girl into her arms. Sally's face was puckered up as though she were going to cry, but instead she began to laugh. "Daddy taught me how to float," she said proudly. "But I sort of forgot how until she," pointing to Honey, "threw me her shirt. I can swim too," she went on, wriggling away from Trixie and dog-paddling the rest of the way to shore just as though she hadn't been on the verge of drowning a minute before. "But," the little girl admitted as she climbed up on the bank again, "I don't like to swim in *deep* water."

Trixie looked at Honey and laughed. "So that's all the thanks you get."

Honey, in her wet vest and shorts, leaned over to twist the water out of her hair. Then she slipped into her shirt, laughing. "It feels fine to be cold for a change, but I think we'd all better go home and put on dry clothes. Do you feel all right, Sally?"

But Sally had already started to trot along the path toward the red trailer. "Course I feel all right," she said over one shoulder. "But I'd better not let Daddy catch me talking to you 'trangers."

"You were wonderful, Honey," Trixie said admiringly as they set off in the opposite direction. "Where did you learn that life-saving trick with a shirt?"

"At camp," Honey told her. "And it's a good one to know about because there's very little danger of being choked or kicked by the person you're trying to rescue. Sally is so young I was sure she'd get panicky and grab me around the neck if I got too close. But there was nothing to that rescue as soon as she turned on her back and floated."

"I wish I were as level-headed as you," Trixie said ruefully. "I got so excited I barged right into the lake with my shoes on." Water sloshed out of her moccasins. "And," she added, "I wish I could swim as well as you do, Honey."

Honey smiled. "If you'd gone to camp as many years as I have, you'd be much better than I am. Look how quickly you learned to ride. Regan thinks you're the best pupil he ever had. You'll be riding circles around me soon."

Trixie flushed with pleasure. "It'll be years before I catch up with you and Jim. You're both marvelous."

Honey, embarrassed, quickly changed the subject.

"That shaggy-haired man couldn't be too mean a father, Trixie," she said. "Not if he went to all the trouble of teaching his little girl to float. And she didn't talk as though she were the least bit afraid of him. I'm beginning to think—" She stopped as they heard footsteps on the path behind them.

Both girls turned around and there, hurrying after them, was Joeanne, her pigtails flying. Cuddled in her arms, as happy as though he belonged there, was the black cocker spaniel puppy.

"Buddy!" Honey gasped. "Then he did follow you?"

Joeanne shook her head soberly as she handed the puppy to Honey. "No. Somehow or other my little sister hid him in the trailer just before we left camp this morning. We didn't find him till we stopped for lunch. I'm awfully sorry it happened."

She turned to go but Honey stopped her with an impulsive gesture. "Oh, don't be sorry," she cried generously. "If Sally loves Buddy that much I think she should have him. I can get another dog. Please, take him back to your little sister."

Joeanne pulled away and set her shoulders stiffly. "No thank you. Sally should be punished for taking him away from you. You must have been awfully worried about him."

44

"But maybe he followed her inside your trailer," Honey pointed out. "I don't think she should be punished. It was our fault for leaving a window open."

Joeanne frowned as though she were holding back hot tears. "I don't think you left a window open," she said evenly. "I think Sally climbed in your trailer and took him. Anyway," she finished in a rush of words, "we can't keep him. We couldn't afford to feed him."

Then before they could stop her, she buried her face in the crook of her arm and stumbled into the woods. Trixie and Honey watched her until she disappeared down a path that wound around the hill and away from where the red trailer was parked.

Chapter 4
An Awkward Moment

The girls put on their bathing suits, took a quick swim in the lake, then dressed in dry playsuits. The roast potatoes Miss Trask had cooked were delicious with the broiled hamburgers and tomatoes. They toasted marsh-mallows on long sticks and ate so many of them Miss Trask said they would be sick.

"I can't get used to Honey's new appetite," she told Trixie. "Before she met you she hardly ate a thing."

Honey smiled, her mouth too full to speak, and Trixie said, "I wonder what the red trailer family had for lunch. They all look half-starved."

"I wish we could do something for them," Honey said. "I couldn't bear it when Joanne stumbled off in the woods crying. What do you suppose makes them so unhappy?"

"I can't understand any of it," Trixie said as she burned the paper plates and wiped the forks with a paper napkin.

They threw dirt on the dying embers of the fire to make sure it was out, then Miss Trask said, "Why don't you two ride in the trailer? Perhaps you could take naps. Nobody had much sleep last night."

"All right," Trixie and Honey agreed, and in a few minutes they were ready to start. They had just got the dogs safely inside when they saw the red trailer coming around the lake. It stopped beside the *Swan* and the shaggy-haired man got out. He walked a few steps toward the girls, then hesitated and turned to go back.

"Hello," Honey called. "Can we do anything for you?"

He wheeled, stared at them for a minute as though trying to make up his mind about something, then came closer.

"Did you see my little girl?" he asked in a queer, low voice. "The one with the black braids?"

"Yes," Honey and Trixie said together. "She brought back the puppy just before lunch."

The man nodded. "We haven't seen her since then. Did you notice where she went?"

"Through the woods," Trixie said, pointing. "We wondered why she went off in the opposite direction from where you were parked."

The man's shoulders slumped. "Then she meant what she said," he sighed, more to himself than to them. "I didn't think she'd do it." His face was expressionless, but he let out a groan of despair as he turned and walked slowly back to the *Robin*. He climbed into the driver's seat, said something to his wife which they couldn't hear, and drove away down the road.

Honey and Trixie stared at each other in amazement. "He's gone off and left her wandering around in the woods," she gasped. "Oh, Trixie, what'll we do?"

"We can't do anything," Trixie said. "We'd never find her in those thick woods, especially since it looks as though she doesn't want to be found!"

Miss Trask called to them from the tow car. "All aboard, you two! We must get started if we want to reach Autoville before dark."

Trixie and Honey climbed aboard the *Swan* and Honey stretched out on the davenport. Trixie clambered up to her bunk.

"You watch from your window," Trixie said. "And I'll watch from mine. Maybe we'll pass Joeanne on the road. If she's run away from her family she may have hidden beside the main highway until she saw the *Robin* go past. It would be easier walking on the road than through the woods."

"But we don't know which direction she'll take," Honey said sadly. "If she goes south we'll never find her."

"Well, she was going north when we saw her last," Trixie pointed out.

"Why do you suppose she ran away, if she did?" Honey wondered out loud.

"The only reason I can think of," Trixie said after thinking for a minute, "is that her father must be so cruel to her she couldn't bear it any longer."

"I don't think he is cruel," Honey broke in. "He didn't look mean when he asked us if we'd seen her back at the lake. He looked—well, sort of beaten. I felt sorry for him."

"Well, I didn't," Trixie said briskly. "He had no business driving off and leaving an eleven-year-old girl."

"I know," Honey argued, "but if Joeanne ran away there was nothing else for him to do. You said yourself nobody could find her in those woods."

"He could notify the police," Trixie said. "That's what our family would do if we ran away and they couldn't wait for us to come back."

"Maybe he did," Honey said. "Maybe he stopped at the next town." She looked relieved at the thought. "The state troopers are probably combing the woods for Joeanne right now."

"I wish I thought so," Trixie said. "They're so wonderful they'd find her right away. But somehow I have a feeling that shaggy-haired man doesn't want to have anything to do with the police. There's something mysterious going on inside that trailer. I'm going to keep watching out the window for Joeanne."

But she didn't. The swim and the big lunch made her so sleepy she couldn't keep her eyes open. When she woke up, they had stopped at the entrance to a large trailer park and Honey was rubbing her eyes and yawning.

"Oh, dear," she sighed ruefully. "We both fell asleep. Here we are at Autoville."

After Miss Trask had made arrangements with the proprietor for space and use of water and electrical connections, she drove the *Swan* down past a long line of parked trailers to the stand she had rented. Trixie and Honey jumped out, followed by the dogs.

"Why, this is a regular resort," Trixie said, staring around her. Every stand had a tiny, flower-bordered lawn of its own, and in the middle of the landscaped park was an enormous swimming pool.

"That's right," Honey said. "Some people live here all the year round. They have oil burners and everything in their trailers."

A uniformed attendant backed the *Swan* into its section of the auto village, and after giving Miss Trask a receipt, drove the tow car off to a parking lot.

"The tow cars," Miss Trask explained, "are parked so you can sit in them and watch the outdoor movies.

And just beyond that area is the riding academy where you girls can rent horses."

"This is going to be fun," Trixie began excitedly and then stopped as a state trooper on a motorcycle appeared at the entrance to Autoville. "Honey," she finished in a gasp. "You were right! He's looking for Joeanne."

After talking to the proprietor, the trooper walked slowly along the road that encircled the park and swimming pool, stopping at each trailer to ask questions. When he arrived at the *Swan,* he said to Miss Trask, "We're searching for a stolen trailer, lady. If you happened to notice a large red one on the road anywhere, it would be a big help. Here are the license numbers."

Miss Trask frowned as he handed her a slip of paper. "I'm not good at remembering numbers," she said.

Trixie, appalled at the thought that Joeanne's family was riding around in a stolen trailer, suddenly felt sorry for the shaggy-haired man. There must be some mistake, she decided. If he had stolen the *Robin* he wouldn't have parked in public camps where he could easily be traced. And people who steal trailers don't go riding around in the open, taking their children with them.

"But," Miss Trask continued to the trooper, "we did see a big red trailer at the picnic grounds about twenty miles north of Poughkeepsie."

"There are lots of red trailers in the world," Trixie said quickly.

"And the one we saw couldn't have been stolen," Honey added. "The man who was driving the tow car had all his family with him."

The trooper shrugged. "Well, I guess that wasn't the one then. This is the fourth trailer theft reported in the last couple of weeks. And in each case we've found the trailer abandoned on a side road a short time after it was stolen."

"How peculiar," Miss Trask said. "Why should anybody steal something and then abandon it?"

The trooper frowned. "Not so peculiar as you might think. Whoever steals these trailers—and we suspect a gang—strips the interiors of everything valuable before he abandons them. People are awfully careless with trailers," he went on. "They're so big and so easily recognized, the owners feel confident nobody would try to steal them any more than a thief would try to steal a house. You'd be surprised how many people leave their keys in the tow car and go off for hours. All the thief has to do is drive into some isolated spot, transfer the trailer equipment to his truck and drive away again." He shrugged in disgust. "The guy who owned the red trailer we're looking for now, left it hitched up, all ready to go, in his garage and left town for a week. He came back sooner than he had planned and now he's yelling, 'Help, help!' to us."

"He certainly invited trouble," Miss Trask agreed. "And I'll be very careful driving back with the *Swan*. Why, the fixtures in it must have cost several thousand dollars!"

"That's right," the trooper said. "The last one we found abandoned was minus a radio, an electric dishwasher, stove and refrigerator, all brand new. There's a smart gang back of these robberies. They haven't attempted to sell any of the loot yet. We figure they'll wait till the excitement dies down, then they'll load up a truck and try to dispose of the stuff in some other state." He tipped his cap and moved on to the next trailer. "Got to keep on with the routine questioning," he said over his shoulder, "but I haven't much hope of finding the *Robin* until after the nest has been robbed."

Miss Trask apparently had not heard him, but Honey and Trixie stared at each other. The *Robin!* Could there be two red trailers with that name?

"Well, girls," Miss Trask said, glancing at her wrist watch, "it's getting late. Let's have dinner in the restaurant. You can start housekeeping in earnest tomorrow."

They strolled around the park to the big cafeteria which was really more of a clubhouse with a recreation room, library, and dance hall. Music was blaring from an electric record player and couples were dancing indoors and out on the wide screened porch. But Trixie hardly saw or heard anything. All she could think of was that the shaggy-haired man had stolen the *Robin* after all. And that meant he wouldn't dare notify the police that Joeanne had run away. Where was the thin little girl now?

Trixie shuddered. It was growing dark, and she must be all alone in the woods, hungry and frightened. Hardly realizing what she was doing, Trixie stacked dishes on her tray and followed Miss Trask and Honey to a table. But before she could reach the table, a waiter with a huge tray of stacked soiled dishes cut directly in front of her. Trixie tried to turn, but people in line behind her had crowded too close, and the waiter's tray crashed right into Trixie's.

Trixie winced as hot spaghetti skidded along her bare arms, and then the stack of soiled dishes toppled to the cement floor with a deafening crash. Somebody near Trixie screamed and a man behind one of the counters yelled, "For Pete's sake, Jeff, that's the second time this week. You're as good as fired."

The waiter scowled and turned on Trixie, spluttering with rage. "It was all your fault. You weren't watching where you were going. You'll have to pay for the damage, you stupid little fool!"

Trixie gulped guiltily. She *had* been lost in thought, but the waiter certainly had no business cutting right in front of her. "I'm sorry," she began but both Miss Trask and the manager had hurried to the scene.

"All right, Jeff, all right, clean up this mess," the manager said briskly.

"We'll be glad to pay for the damage," Miss Trask told him.

"It wasn't the girl's fault at all," a man behind Trixie put in. "That waiter is a clumsy oaf."

Jeff's face reddened and he shook one fist threateningly as he shouted, "The customer's always right, but I'm not going to pay for this wreckage. You can't make me."

Miss Trask slipped a bill from her purse but the manager waved it away. "That's very kind of you, miss," he said, "but I happened to see the whole thing and the young lady was not in the least to blame." He added in an undertone to Jeff, "When you've cleaned up this mess come into my office. I've had about all the complaints I can take about you."

Jeff darted a malicious glance at Trixie, but set to work obeying the manager's orders. Later when things had quieted down, he passed close behind her chair on his way to the office. "I'll get back at you for this," he hissed. "Just wait and see."

Trixie flushed, and Honey said quickly, "Don't pay any attention to him."

"But I can't help feeling guilty," Trixie said. "I'm not sure it wasn't partly my fault. I think I'd feel better if the manager let me pay for some of that broken china."

"Very well," Miss Trask said. "Go and speak to him after dinner, but let's eat now while things are hot."

When she had finished her pie and ice cream, Trixie pushed back her chair. "You don't need to wait for me. I'll meet you back at the *Swan.*"

"I'll come with you," Honey offered, and the two girls left the cafeteria together. They hurried across the lobby to the offices in the back. Trixie knocked on the door marked *Manager,* and it was opened by the manager himself.

"I'd like to pay—" Trixie began, but he interrupted her with a smile and an apology.

"That man Jeff has a quick temper, but he is very much ashamed of himself. I'm sorry there was such an unpleasant scene. It won't happen again, I assure you."

He bowed the girls out of the room and closed the door before Trixie could protest. "Well, that's that," she told Honey. "But I don't think Jeff is the least bit ashamed of himself. He's as mad at me as he can be."

They walked out of a side door to the veranda and waited for a minute to let their eyes get accustomed to the darkness before starting down the steps. From the shadows under the trees on the lawn came the sound of angry whispering, "You fool! Watch your step or you'll get fired."

"I tell you it wasn't my fault," someone whined defensively. "And I'm getting sick of toting dirty dishes all day long. Why don't we swap jobs?"

Trixie clutched Honey's arm. They had both recognized the whining voice. It was Jeff's!

"Swap jobs," the other voice whispered derisively. "You haven't got the skill to do my work. You're too clumsy and you know it." A man moved out of the shadows and across the lawn. As he passed through the patch of light in front of the cafeteria Trixie saw that he was about the same height and weight as Joeanne's father and had a crop of thick bushy hair. Then he disappeared into the shadows again. In a minute Jeff came out from under the trees and hurried through the back door of the restaurant.

Trixie and Honey went slowly down the steps and around the park. "It gets more and more mysterious every minute," Trixie said. "Do you think the man Jeff was talking to is Joeanne's father?"

"It certainly looked like him," Honey said. "And what do you suppose they were talking about?"

"It didn't make any sense to me," Trixie admitted. "I'm all mixed up and so worried about that poor little girl all alone in the woods I can't think straight."

"Neither can I," Honey agreed. "The only good part of it is that while we're looking for Jim we can look for her at the same time."

"That's true," Trixie said, cheering up a little. "Oh, Honey, we've just got to find them both!"

Chapter 5
On Jim's Trail

The next morning after breakfast Miss Trask spread out her map and marked the trails they should take to Pine Hollow Camp.

"You can't possibly get lost," she told them. "At least not for long. All the bridle paths, you see, come out sooner or later onto one of the main highways. And those routes converge at a point about a mile north of here. The worst that can happen to you is that you may keep riding in circles."

"Neither one of us has any sense of direction," Trixie laughed. "So just in case, let's take along a picnic lunch."

"Wonderful," Honey agreed.

They made thick sandwiches of ham and cheese and filled a Thermos with iced cocoa. Then they set off for the riding academy. Trixie, who hadn't been riding very long, wisely chose a quiet black horse named Prince. "I'm not taking any chances," she said with a grin. "If we get into trouble, Miss Trask might make us go right back home."

"You're right," Honey said as she swung up on the back of a more frisky chestnut gelding named Peanuts. "I'm scared to death Mother may change her mind any minute and call the cafeteria saying she doesn't want me riding around in the woods without an armed guard."

"It must be an awful nuisance being rich," Trixie said as they trotted along the path to the woods. "Your parents are always worrying for fear you'll be kidnaped and held for ransom, aren't they?"

"They used to be," Honey said, "before Miss Trask came. She told Dad she thought it would be better to risk being kidnaped than to grow up different from other girls."

Trixie laughed. "Well, nobody would suspect you're rich now. Your blue jeans are as faded as Joeanne's and look at those big patches on the knees."

"That's where I ripped them when I fell off your bike," Honey said with a giggle. "I put those patches on myself and I'm very proud of them."

"Jim's dungarees were faded and patched too," Trixie suddenly remembered. "He didn't have a stitch of clothes except the ones he was wearing."

"But he's got all that money you saved from the fire," Honey pointed out. "I wonder if he still has his silver christening mug and the old family Bible that had the will in it."

"What I'm wondering," Trixie said, "is where he sleeps nights. That is, if he hasn't already got a job at one of the boys' camps."

"Why, he could go to a hotel, couldn't he?" Honey demanded.

Trixie shook her head. "Not without arousing suspicion. Boys his age don't go around stopping at hotels."

"I never thought about that," Honey said slowly. "He can't spend a lot of money in any one place either without making people think he might have stolen it."

"That's the trouble," Trixie said. "When you get right down to it, Jim has to get a job right away. And it's got to be some place where he can live too."

"Well, let's hope we find him at Pine Hollow," Honey said.

They cantered along in silence until the trail ended at a macadam road. "Now," Honey said, reining in her horse, "we go north, don't we, and pick up the bridle path again in a few yards?"

"I think so," Trixie said. "It looks so easy on the map, but when you get here it's something else again."

They walked their horses along the highway and suddenly Honey called out, "There's the trail and look, aren't we lucky? There's a sign saying it's the one to Pine Hollow!"

Half an hour later they galloped up a hill and found themselves looking down at a large camp that sprawled around a lake. There were several small cabins and one large one nestling among the pine trees, and the lake was dotted with boys in swimming.

"That's it all right," Trixie cried as they started down the hill.

Halfway down they met a group on horseback riding up the winding trail. "Hello," Trixie called to the young counselor who was leading the way. "We were coming down to see you. We're looking for a friend of ours, a boy named Jim."

The counselor grinned. "We have three boys named Jim in camp. Which one is your friend?"

"The red-haired one." Honey laughed.

All the boys grinned then. "Two of 'em have red hair. Take your choice."

Trixie flushed with embarrassment. "I started out all wrong," she said. "The Jim we're looking for wouldn't be a camper. He's trying to get a job as junior counselor or athletic instructor."

"Oh, that's different," the young man said. "A red-haired boy of about fifteen did apply for a job day before yesterday. He didn't say what his name was, but he was riding a bicycle. Does that help you any?"

Trixie looked at Honey. Jim might have bought a bike, she decided, and said out loud, "I guess that's the one. Did he get a job with you?"

The counselor shook his head. "No, there aren't any positions open at Pine Hollow. It's too bad. He looked like a nice kid, and a husky one."

"He didn't say where he was going, did he?" Honey asked.

The counselor shook his head. "No, he just rode right off on his bike toward the main highway."

The girls gathered up their reins and turned their horses around. "Well, thanks a lot, anyway," Trixie said with a wave of good-by.

Honey pulled Peanuts off the path. "Don't you want to go ahead?" she asked the boys. "We've got to walk our horses for a while. They're too hot."

"Thanks," the counselor said and led his group at a canter up the hill.

Trixie watched them disappear around a bend in the trail. "Anyway," she said, "now we know that we were right about Jim. He *is* trying to get a job at one of the camps. Maybe he'll be at Wilson Ranch when we get there tomorrow."

"I hope so," Honey said as they started back. "If only we knew where he's living!"

"I can guess," Trixie said.

"Where?" Honey turned in the saddle to stare at Trixie.

"Right in the woods," Trixie told her. "It would be the safest place. He's so smart he could make himself a wonderful camp and be as snug as a bug in a rug."

"I guess you're right," Honey said thoughtfully. "But I hope he didn't try to sleep outdoors during that awful rain night before last."

"Jim wouldn't have minded that at all," Trixie said. "He could have rigged up some sort of waterproof shelter. I bet he's built a swell shack by now. Oh, golly," she interrupted herself suddenly. "Where are the dogs? I forgot all about them!"

"Oh, gosh." Honey sighed. "So did I. They raced ahead of us along the path when we left the riding academy, but I don't remember seeing them since."

"Neither do I," Trixie admitted. "Maybe they decided not to come along and found their way back to the trailer camp."

"I guess that's what happened," Honey said.

As if in answer to her thoughts, Reddy suddenly bounded across the trail with Bud behind him, and disappeared in the underbrush.

"Well, I like that!" Trixie said in exasperation.

"They were so busy hunting something they didn't even see us." She began to whistle and call but the dogs did not come back.

"Oh, let's leave them," Honey said after a while. "They can probably find their way back to Autoville better than we can."

"Okay," Trixie agreed. "As a matter of fact, I'm sort of confused and mixed up. Do we take the left or the right fork here?"

Honey reined in her horse and gazed down at the intersection of the two paths. "Oh, oh," she gasped. "Do you see what I see? Bicycle tracks! Maybe they'll lead us to Jim."

Trixie slid out of the saddle. "You're right," she said slowly. "But this couldn't be the same path we just rode up. If it was, our horses would have stamped out all signs of the tire treads." She swung up on Prince's back. "We're sure to get lost, but let's go!"

Honey giggled. "I think this is the trail we should have taken in the first place. The other one wound round and round instead of going straight to Pine Hollow."

"This is a real road," Trixie agreed.

"Oh, I'm so excited at the thought of seeing Jim again I can hardly bear it," Honey said. "And you know what? This is something I didn't dare tell you before because I

wasn't sure we'd ever find any trace of Jim. But when I told Miss Trask how much you and I liked him and how wonderful it would be if he could come and live with us, and he and I could go to school in Sleepyside with you and your brothers, she said it was a wonderful idea."

"It is a wonderful idea," Trixie said. "I can't stop thinking about it."

"I can't either," Honey said. "So I wrote to Mother and Dad air mail before we left, telling them all about Jim and asking them if they would adopt him. Of course, I haven't had time to hear yet, but I might get a letter tomorrow."

"Oh, Honey," Trixie gasped. "Do you think they'll do it?"

"Miss Trask seemed to think so," Honey said. "She and Mr. Rainsford talked about it for a long time on Thursday after you went home. At first he wanted to adopt Jim himself but he travels a lot all over the world, so he wouldn't be a very good father. And Miss Trask argued that Jim ought to grow up with other boys and girls. So finally he said he'd write to Dad himself about appointing him as guardian, anyway. They're old friends, you know. As a matter of fact, Mr. Rainsford suddenly remembered that Dad and Jim's father knew each other years ago. They went to the same school or something."

"It's getting better and better," Trixie cried enthusiastically. "How do you think your mother will feel about adopting Jim?"

"I—don't—know," Honey admitted ruefully. "I'm scared she won't even consider it. But somehow I feel sure if she could meet Jim she would like him as much as we do." Tears welled up in her wide hazel eyes. "When I was little I heard my nurse talking to the cook and she said the reason my mother didn't pay any attention to me was because I was a girl instead of a boy."

"How perfectly awful," Trixie exploded. "And of course it's not true. You should never have paid any attention to such silly talk."

Honey looked down at her long slender hands for a moment. "Well, anyway, if Mother does want a son, she couldn't find anybody better than Jim. And he's a lot like Dad. You know, they both have quick tempers, like most redheaded people, but they never stay mad long. And they're terribly frank and honest and athletic and love the outdoors." She smiled suddenly through her tears. "I'll probably be terribly jealous of Jim if Dad does adopt him."

Trixie laughed. "Jim is just what you need to help you get to know your parents. The only trouble with you and your mother is that you're both shy. But Jim isn't. Remember the day we discovered him? We felt as though we'd known him all our lives in just a few minutes."

The trail ended abruptly at the macadam road, several yards north of the winding path they had taken earlier to Pine Hollow.

"Now what?" Trixie asked. "Did Jim go north or south on the highway, or did he pick up the trail on the other side of the road?"

Honey stared down at the faint marks of bicycle tire treads in the dirt. "Your guess is as good as mine," she said. "But let's ride north for a bit and see if there is another path leading into the woods."

"Maybe he cut through this underbrush," Trixie wondered out loud. "It looks as though somebody might have dragged a bike through here recently."

"Well, we can't go that way," Honey objected. "Not on horseback."

A twig crackled and both girls turned quickly, just in time to catch a glimpse of something that looked like blue jeans disappearing in the thicket.

"Jim," both girls gasped at once, then raised their voices. "Jim! Jim!" they shouted.

And then the dogs came bounding down the trail. A few feet from the road, Reddy suddenly swerved, and, barking joyfully as though greeting an old friend, tore off through the underbrush, with Bud.

"It *was* Jim," Trixie said. "Reddy recognized him."

"I don't think so," Honey objected. "He would have answered us. And Reddy thinks everybody's his best friend. So does Bud."

Trixie looked discouraged. "We couldn't possibly be lucky enough to find Jim the very first thing," she said. "I guess whoever was wearing those dungarees is a Pine Hollow boy exploring the woods."

"That's what I think," Honey said. "Let's try to find another path with more bicycle marks on it."

They rode up the highway for half a mile or so but saw no more bridle paths. They were just about to turn back when a large van came lumbering out of the woods just ahead of them.

"There must be a road there," Trixie cried excitedly. "Let's see if there are any signs of tire treads."

As they passed the van, Trixie glanced disinterestedly at the driver, but a second later, she sucked in her breath and whispered to Honey, "The man driving that van had bushy hair, like Joeanne's father, and the other one looked like Jeff, the waiter!"

Honey turned in the saddle to stare after the van. "Are you sure?" she demanded. "I mean, are you sure it was Joeanne's father?"

Trixie shook her head. "No. His face was turned away from me, but he had that same shaggy hair. I could hardly see the other man he was talking to but he did look like Jeff."

"Well, a lot of people have bushy hair," Honey said, "and a lot of people look like Jeff. You know, neither tall nor short, not fat or thin, and sort of colorless eyes and hair." She giggled. "All waiters look alike to me anyway."

"Say," Trixie interrupted in amazement. "This isn't a road that van came out of. It's just a cleared space between the trees and the bushes."

"I guess the driver thought it was a road," Honey said, "and turned in by mistake."

"But then," Trixie argued, "he would have backed out. There's no room to turn here. And he was headed toward the highway."

"That's true," Honey said thoughtfully.

"And look!" Trixie shouted in excitement as she slipped out of the saddle. "Just look at this pile of branches. They must have been used to camouflage the van so nobody passing by would notice it."

Honey jumped down beside her. On one side of the clearing, bushy evergreens were heaped high. On closer inspection they discovered folded neatly nearby an old tennis court net.

Honey was completely mystified, but Trixie yelled, "I get it. Don't you see? They back the van in here and cover it with branches. Then they stretch this net between the trees facing the road on either side of the clearing. After that all they have to do to hide the van completely is wind more branches through the holes in the net. It makes a perfect screen so nobody would ever guess there was a van parked in this patch of woods."

"Then," Honey said slowly, "those two men must be the trailer thieves. They carry away in the van the stuff they steal. Oh, I hate to think of Joeanne's father being arrested, but we really ought to tell the state troopers just as soon as possible."

"We can't do that yet," Trixie argued. "We're not sure the driver of the van was Joeanne's father, and how do we know this really is a hideaway? Let's come back some other time when the van is hidden here. If we see trailer equipment inside it then we'll have proof."

Honey shuddered. "But suppose they catch us spying on them, Trixie? That Jeff is awfully mean-tempered and he has it in for you anyway."

Trixie shrugged. "I'm not afraid of him, but I am starving. Let's eat."

"Not here," Honey protested, looking over her shoulder. "Those men might come back."

"All right," Trixie agreed. "It would be better to ride down to the path where we found the bicycle tracks and have a picnic lunch near there. We might find some more clues to where Jim is."

73

Chapter 6
An Eavesdropper

As they rode a little way up the Pine Hollow trail again, the dogs came dashing out of the woods. They were both dripping wet and sprayed the girls with water.

"They've been in swimming, the lucky dogs." Trixie laughed. "There must be a brook near here. Let's try to find it so we can wash up before lunch."

"But we can't take the horses through that thick underbrush," Honey objected. "They might get badly scratched or stumble and go lame. I wouldn't worry so much if Prince and Peanuts belonged to us, but we'd better not take any chances with rented horses."

"You're right." Trixie sighed. "But I'm just dying to explore in there. Suppose those blue jeans we saw belonged to Jim?"

"I'm sure they didn't." Honey handed Trixie a sandwich and unscrewed the top of the Thermos. "Even if he didn't hear us call, he would have recognized Reddy and known we were near. He wouldn't run away from us, Trixie."

"I'm not so sure of that," Trixie said. "Maybe something's happened so he feels he has to hide from everyone. We haven't seen a newspaper since we left home. Suppose a reporter discovered Jim didn't die in the fire after all? There would be another front-page story about the missing heir, and Jonesy would start looking for Jim again."

"Oh, golly," Honey groaned. "I can't bear to think of anything so awful happening. If Jonesy should find Jim before we do, he'll beat him and tie him up the way he did the time Jim ran away before."

"Jim will never let that happen," Trixie said. "And that's what worries me. We shouldn't waste any more time. Let's ride to Wilson Ranch this afternoon and see if he got a job there."

Honey glanced up at the sky. "We would never be able to make it before it rains. It's going to pour any minute. We ought to start for home right away."

Sure enough, it was already sprinkling when the girls returned their horses to the riding academy, and they had to run all the way to the *Swan* to keep from getting soaked. The rain kept up a steady drumming on the roof of the trailer all day, and the girls were forced to play indoor games and read, but it was hard to control their impatience.

At last Trixie said restlessly, "I can't stand being

cooped up here any longer. Let's dash over to the restaurant and play some Ping-Pong before dinner."

"All right," Miss Trask agreed. "I'll take a nap, but wear your slickers and rubbers. If either of you should catch cold it would ruin the trip."

"We won't," Honey assured her. "And please don't let the dogs follow us. They've already brought in so much mud Trixie and I'll have to spend most of the morning scrubbing the place."

They raced around the park in their oilskin capes and hoods and sloshed up the steps to the cafeteria veranda. Everybody in Autoville seemed to have gathered inside and out of the clubhouse, and people were waiting in line for the use of the Ping-Pong table.

"Oh dear," Trixie complained. "There's nothing to do here either. I wish we could fall asleep and not wake up until it's time to start looking for Jim tomorrow morning."

Honey was examining a magazine at the newsstand. "This quiz test looks like fun," she said. "Let's find out how smart we are." She bought two copies of the magazine and Trixie followed her to a quiet corner of the library. "Ready, get set, go," Honey said. "The one who gets through first and has the most right answers is the smartest."

Trixie scribbled a few answers in the blank spaces after the questions in the test, but in a short while her thoughts began to wander. "I always get sleepy on rainy days," she yawned, bored. "Wish I'd stayed back at the *Swan* with Miss Trask and taken a nap."

"I'm sleepy too," Honey admitted. "Let's doze right here in these comfortable chairs. We can finish the quiz later."

It seemed to Trixie that she had hardly closed her eyes when she was awakened by the sound of whispering on the other side of the thin beaver-board wall that separated the library from one of the back rooms in the cafeteria.

"—abandoned barn," someone was saying, "on that truck farm. Perfectly safe. Hasn't been used in years. Doubt if the farmer even remembers it's there."

"You're taking an awful chance," came a whining whisper. "We were better off where we were."

Trixie sat up. That voice, she felt sure, belonged to Jeff!

"Don't be stupid," the other voice said hoarsely. "Those kids rode into the clearing after we passed them on the highway. If they saw that net and guessed—"

"Those dumb kids!" Jeff snorted. "They wouldn't suspect anything even if they did happen to notice the net. What do you think they are, state troopers?"

"I'm taking no chances," the other man insisted. "They didn't look dumb to me and you could tell by the way they were riding along, watching the side of the road, they were looking for something."

"Oh, all right," Jeff gave in. "But it beats me how you're going to get to that barn without being seen by the farmer who owns it. That van's not exactly small, in case you haven't noticed."

"I keep telling you," the other man whispered impatiently. "Through the back fields. There's an old road leading from the orchard to the barn."

"And fine shape it'll be in after this rain," Jeff argued. "We're sure to get stuck in the mud tonight; but have it your own way. I'll play along, but it sure gets my goat that a couple of clumsy girls can make us change our plans."

The two men moved away from the wall, and in a few seconds Trixie saw the silhouette of a bushy-haired man move furtively past the library window. She hurried to the veranda, straining her eyes to get a better glimpse of him. He turned as though he might have heard her tiptoeing after him, and she crouched down hastily behind a bench. Peeking through the slats in the back of the bench, Trixie held her breath as the man

took a few steps in her direction. Then, jamming a battered hat down over his thick, unruly hair, he wheeled
and vaulted over the porch railing to disappear in the
shadows of the bushes.

It was dark on the veranda, for due to the rain the
outside lights had not been turned on, but Trixie had
seen enough of the man's face to feel sure that he was
not Joeanne's father. Hastily she returned to the library
and woke Honey to tell her what had happened.

"I can't be absolutely sure, of course," she finished,
"but he didn't have that sort of vacant look that the red
trailer man had. He didn't look beaten at all; he had
sharp features and narrow eyes and with all that bushy
hair he made me think of a fox."

"Well, Joeanne's father doesn't look anything like a
fox," Honey said. "The last time I saw him he reminded
me of a great big, sad-eyed dog that didn't have any
home. Even if he did go off and leave Joeanne, I feel
sorry for him."

"Honey!" Trixie gasped. "You've hit the nail on the
head. That's just what's wrong with that family—why
they look so vacant, as though they had given up hope.
They haven't any home."

"They've got the red trailer," Honey began and then
stopped. "Oh, I see what you mean. They must have stolen

the trailer because they haven't any other place to live."

"That's it," Trixie cried. "If you had all those children and no home for them and you saw a trailer all hitched up and ready to go, wouldn't you be tempted?"

Honey nodded her head up and down sympathetically. "The man who owns the *Robin* shouldn't have gone off and left his keys in the tow car. It serves him right, and I'm glad we didn't tell the state trooper anything."

"We didn't have anything to tell him," Trixie pointed out, "except that we saw a red trailer at the picnic grounds, and Miss Trask told him that."

Honey sighed. "I hope we never run across that poor family again. If we should see the *Robin* while we're looking for Jim we'd have to notify the police, wouldn't we? I mean, if the father is a thief, it wouldn't be right to withhold information that would lead to his arrest."

"Well, anyway," Trixie said, "he's not the same thief who's been stealing trailer equipment. If you ask me, Jeff and his bushy-haired friend have something to do with those robberies."

"It certainly looks like it," Honey said thoughtfully. "A hidden van and all that talk you just heard about an abandoned barn! Shouldn't we tell the troopers what we suspect?"

"It wouldn't do any good," Trixie told her. "I gather they're not going to hide the van in the woods any more. And we haven't the vaguest idea where the abandoned barn is. We've got to get some proof before we can report anything to the police. If I told them I suspected Jeff, they'd think I was trying to get him into trouble because he bumped into me with a tray of dishes."

"Oh, golly," Honey moaned. "It seems to me we've got too many things to do in such a short time. We want to find Jim and Joeanne, and we don't want to find the red trailer, and at the same time we ought to be looking for that van and an abandoned barn."

Trixie laughed. "We don't really *have* to do anything but find Jim, but I hope we find Joeanne too. I can't bear the thought of that poor little girl wandering around all by herself."

"Maybe she isn't any more," Honey said without much hope. "Maybe she knew where her family was going in the trailer and has caught up with them by now."

Trixie shook her head. "Then why did she run away in the first place?"

"I don't know," Honey began and then she said with a little gasp, "Oh, Trixie, did you ever think that the person in faded blue jeans who disappeared into the woods back at the Pine Hollow trail might have been Joeanne?

Both the dogs know her pretty well, and especially Bud!"

Trixie's mouth fell open in amazement. "We don't need a quiz test to prove who's the smartest," she said ruefully. "I never thought about that, Honey, and I'll bet it *was* Joeanne. Let's go back there and explore some more as soon as we can."

"You mean tomorrow as soon as we've cleaned up the *Swan?*" Honey demanded. "Don't you think we'd better ride to Wilson Ranch first? We don't want to lose track of Jim."

"Of course not," Trixie agreed. "We'll look for clues to Joeanne in the afternoon."

Miss Trask beckoned to them from the doorway then, and they hurried to follow her into the diningroom. As they stood in line with their trays in the cafeteria, the radio began to blare forth the latest news and weather reports.

"Upstate," the announcer in the New York broadcasting station said, "police are searching for a gang of trailer thieves. Three of the four stolen trailers have already been located only a short distance from where their owners left them, stripped of all valuable and movable equipment. But so far state troopers have found no trace of the luxury trailer, named the *Robin.*" The announcer repeated several times the license plates on the *Robin* and on the tow car and then issued the warning, "All trailer owners are cautioned against parking in side roads or in the woods and are especially urged not to abandon their homes-on-wheels at any time unless they are parked in supervised trailer camps."

"This whole business is making me rather nervous," Miss Trask said when they were seated at a table. "I feel terribly responsible for the *Swan*. If anything should happen to it, I'd never forgive myself, although I suppose it is heavily insured."

"And it's perfectly safe while we're in Autoville," Honey said quickly.

"Nevertheless," Miss Trask told her, "I'd like to take it back home as soon as possible. You two can inquire for Jim at Wilson Ranch tomorrow and at Rushkill Farms on Tuesday. Then I think we ought to make an early start for Sleepyside Wednesday morning."

Honey and Trixie stared at each other in dismay. Only two more days, and they had so much to do!

Honey immediately began to plead for more time, but Trixie had suddenly caught sight of the waiter, Jeff. He was clearing the soiled dishes from a table which some young people had just vacated, but he was working so slowly, stacking the plates with exaggerated care, wiping carefully at unseen spots, that Trixie became suspicious. And then she realized that he was listening to every word a man and woman at the next table were saying.

The middle-aged couple had a map spread out in front of them, and while they sipped after-dinner coffee, they were discussing plans for a trip.

"We can stop here for a swim before lunch," the man told his wife, pointing with a pencil. "That's a lake, see? I get so hot driving in the heat of the day, I'd welcome a chance to cool off."

The woman smiled. "Then why do we leave Autoville at all? There's a lovely pool right here, Rob."

Her husband chuckled. "You know perfectly well, Anna, that I've got to combine business with pleasure on my vacation. I must get that client in Tookerstown to sign the contract sometime this week. You don't have to come with me if you'd prefer to stay here."

"Of course I want to come," his wife said quickly. "But is it necessary to take the trailer? I'm sort of nervous since those robberies."

"It's not necessary," the man said, "but a lot more comfortable. We can eat whenever we like and change into bathing suits without having to look for bathhouses. Tookerstown is just a small village on a country road, and I doubt if we'll pass an inn on the way."

His wife laughed as they left the table. "We could,

of course, take sandwiches but I guess I've spoiled you with my home cooking."

Trixie pretended to eat but she was watching Jeff out of the corner of one eye. As soon as the couple left the cafeteria, he flipped a notebook out of his pocket and wrote something down in it.

So, Trixie thought, *that's why he works in this restaurant. He listens to people's plans so he knows just where they are going to park their trailers when they go on trips. I hope that man doesn't leave his keys in the tow car when he and his wife go swimming. I'd like to warn him but I know he'd only laugh at me.*

Later that evening when she was telling her suspicions to Honey, she said, "If only I could get hold of Jeff's notebook! That would be all we needed to prove he's one of the trailer thieves."

Honey thought for a minute. "I don't think any more trailers are going to be stolen for quite a while. Everybody's going to be extra careful after those radio warnings. We simply mustn't waste any more time on that mystery. Let the state troopers worry about it. We've only got two more days to look for Jim and then we'll have to go home."

Trixie sighed. "Is Miss Trask still determined to go home on Wednesday?"

Honey nodded. "She's pretty nervous about it all and feels that when the gang discovers people are being careful of where they park their trailers, they'll try some other way of getting them. Like hijacking."

"Hijacking?" Trixie's blue eyes grew round. "You mean hold up the drivers with guns and force them into the woods and tie them up while they steal the equipment?"

"Miss Trask didn't come right out and say that," Honey admitted. "But that's what *I* think will happen." She shuddered. "I hope the troopers catch that gang before we start back, and I tell you I'm not going to investigate any abandoned barns."

Trixie giggled. "We probably won't have a chance to unless there's one on the Wilson Ranch."

It had stopped raining during dinner and now the moon was shining palely through a veil of clouds. "Let's sit out on the step for a while before we go to bed," Trixie said. "I don't feel a bit sleepy now."

Miss Trask had stayed behind at the cafeteria to talk with some friends she had made while the girls were out riding that morning. "I'd like to go for a swim," Honey said as they strolled past the pool. "But I guess it's too late for that."

They covered the wet step of the *Swan* with

their raincoats and sat down to wait for Miss Trask. Suddenly Trixie grabbed Honey's arm.

"Quick," she whispered. "Look at that man in the Autoville uniform on the other side of the pool."

Honey stared across the park. "What about him? He's just one of the attendants."

"I know," Trixie said, "but just a minute ago he took off his cap to shake the water out of it, and I wish you could have seen his hair. It's as bushy as a fox's tail!"

Honey blinked. "Do you think he's the man whom you heard talking to Jeff before dinner?"

"That one wasn't in uniform," Trixie said, "but, of course, he wouldn't be when he was off duty."

Honey stood up, shivering. "Let's go inside," she begged. "He might have seen you on the veranda when you were spying on him."

Trixie frowned. "I wish he'd turn around so we could see his face."

"Well, I don't," Honey said, opening the *Swan* door. "I don't want to have anything to do with those trailer thieves."

Trixie reluctantly followed her inside. "Somehow," she said slowly, "I feel we aren't going to find either Jim or Joeanne until that mystery is solved."

Chapter 7
Wilson Ranch

The next morning was hot and sunny after the rain, so hot that Trixie felt cross and tired when she and Honey had finished cleaning the interior of the *Swan*. They swept and dusted and mopped for what seemed like hours and it was almost ten o'clock when Miss Trask said the job was done to her satisfaction.

"Let's never take the dogs with us again," Honey said. "They're always running away and they brought in most of the mud and burrs that were stuck to everything."

"They are awful nuisances," Trixie agreed. "May we leave them with you, Miss Trask?"

Miss Trask nodded. "Why don't you take along bathing suits? You may be invited for a swim at the ranch. I understand there is a lovely natural pool, an old quarry, at that boys' camp. The water should be fresh and cold after the rain yesterday."

"Great," Trixie said. "The way I feel now I'd like to stay in the water all day long."

"Me too." Honey rolled their suits into a tight ball

and strapped them together with a belt she could hook to her saddle. "Shall we take lunch too?"

"Oh, let's not," Trixie groaned. "I ate so many pancakes for breakfast I don't ever want to see food again."

"It's only an hour's ride to Wilson Ranch," Miss Trask told them. "You should be back before one. When I take the dogs for a walk, I'll stop at one of the truck farms near here and buy greens for a salad. That, with canned ham broiled with slices of pineapple, and buttered rolls will make a delicious and easy-to-fix dinner."

"Yummy-yum," Trixie cried, completely forgetting that she had just said she never wanted to eat again. "Let's go."

In a few minutes they were riding Prince and Peanuts through a wooded path that led in the opposite direction from the one they had taken to Pine Hollow Camp.

After a while Honey said musingly, "What did you mean, Trixie, when you said last night that we weren't going to find Jim until the trailer-theft mystery was solved?"

Trixie shrugged. "I don't know exactly why, but somehow I have a feeling that Jim isn't at any of those boys' camps, that he's hiding out in the woods. And Joeanne is probably lost in the woods around here and the trailer thieves are hiding in the woods too, and so I keep thinking if we find one of them we'll find all of them."

Honey laughed. "That doesn't make much sense. The woods stretch for miles and miles on each side of the main highway. It would be like trying to find a whole book of needles in one huge haystack."

"I know it." Trixie grinned, and then she sobered. "Say, Honey," she cried, pointing. "Look down there in that hollow. If that isn't an old orchard I never saw one."

Honey reined in Peanuts. "Are those gnarled and tired-looking things apple trees?"

"That's right," Trixie told her. "We have lots of them like that at home. Dad is always going to chop them down for firewood but they are so beautiful when they blossom in the spring Mother won't let him." She leaned across her saddle to whisper, "Do you suppose it's the same orchard Jeff and his bushy-haired friend were talking about?"

Honey shuddered. "If it is, let's not go near the place. I'm scared of those men, Trixie, and they already suspect us of spying on them."

Trixie ignored her. "When we get to the top of this hill, let's look down and see if we can see an old barn. There must be a truck farm around there but the woods shut out our view."

But the trail to Wilson Ranch led downhill instead of up, and Trixie was so busy slapping at the deer flies swarming around Prince's neck that she forgot to look for signs of a farm. The flies left them at the edge of the woods and they cantered across a wide field to pick up the trail again on the other side. They stopped for a cool drink at a spring and bathed their hot arms and faces.

"Whew!" Trixie gasped, as the horses drank thirstily. "This is awful. How much farther do we have to go?"

Honey consulted the map. "Why, we're almost there. As a matter of fact, we are there. This patch of woods belongs to the camp. We should be able to see the cabins in a few minutes."

But before they saw the camp they heard unmistakable sounds of boys in swimming—splashing, yelling, the blowing of a whistle, and then they rounded a bend in the path and found themselves a few yards from the quarry.

One tall, blond boy was poised on the diving board, and Honey cried, "Why, that's my cousin, Ben Riker. I haven't seen him in ages, but I'd know him anywhere. Nobody else is such a clown."

Ben, pretending that he had lost his nerve, was backing away from the edge of the board. All of a sudden he lost his balance and fell over the side with a loud splash. Grinning and spluttering, he emerged and promptly caught sight of the girls and their horses.

"Honey Wheeler!" he shouted, scrambling up the bank. "Where did you come from and what are you doing here?"

Honey introduced him to Trixie and explained about the trailer trip. "We're looking for a redheaded boy named Jim," she said. "Would you know if he tried to get a job at Wilson Ranch?"

"No," Ben said, "but Mr. Ditmar would. He's the tall guy over there blowing the whistle. He owns the joint and is a swell person. Come on, we'll ask him about your friend."

Mr. Ditmar nodded pleasantly when Honey asked him about Jim. "Why, yes," he said, "a husky young redhead applied for a job here yesterday in all that rain. I liked the boy's looks and we could use another junior athletic instructor here for the nursery group, but I couldn't hire anyone without references. A letter from his principal or the minister of his church would do. I told him to have his parents get in touch with me right away."

Honey looked at Trixie. "Oh, gosh," she said under her breath. "That's too bad."

"What do you mean, too bad?" Ben demanded. "He couldn't get a job at a better camp."

"I think I know what she means," Mr. Ditmar said easily. "I got the impression from the way the boy evaded my questions that he was a runaway. Was I right?"

Trixie hesitated a moment, then, deciding that Mr. Ditmar would prove to be a friend, she blurted, "Yes. Jim ran away from his cruel stepfather and we've got to find him before he runs away for good. He's recently inherited half a million dollars but he doesn't know it."

Together the two girls told the whole story, and when they had finished Mr. Ditmar said sympathetically, "I'm sorry now I didn't hire him right on the spot although, of course, I couldn't without knowing more of his background."

"Say," Ben put in, "you girls look as though you were about to have a sunstroke. Would it be all right for them to take a quick swim, Mr. Ditmar?"

"Certainly," Mr. Ditmar said, and added, "We're getting ready for the senior races. Maybe you'd like to stay and watch and have lunch with us afterward. The boys are brewing a hunter's stew back at the ranch house and I'm sure they'd like to try it out on you girls."

Honey giggled. "It sounds like fun but I hope Ben

didn't have anything to do with the stew. If he did I'll bet it's full of red pepper."

"I'll have you know," Ben said airily, "that I'm a better cook than you'll ever be."

"Maybe so," Honey said warily, "but I can't help remembering that hunt breakfast at Grandmother's when you filled all the sugar bowls with salt. Were you ever unpopular!"

"Kid stuff." Ben grinned. "I was knee-high to a grasshopper then," he told Trixie, "but Honey has never forgiven me 'cause her governess made her eat every bit of that salty, salty oatmeal."

"It was a mean trick," Honey insisted, "and I didn't dare tell on him because he said he'd put toads in my bed if I did."

One of Ben's chums who had been standing nearby said with a chuckle, "Riker's a dangerous character, all right, but last night we paid him back for all the stunts he's pulled since camp opened. Didn't we, Ben, old boy?"

Ben clasped his forehead in mock despair. "I'll say you did. I still can't get the knots out of my sheets, and you, a pal of mine, Sid!" He turned to Honey. "Sid and I'll stable your horses while you girls change at the ranch house. Here comes Mrs. Ditmar now. She'll take care of you."

A plump, motherly-looking woman led Honey and Trixie past the stable and the corral to the main house. "I'm glad you brought your bathing suits," she said. "You can change in my room. The telephone is out in the hall if you want to call for permission to stay to lunch."

Honey telephoned the Autoville cafeteria and left a message for Miss Trask with the manager. Then both girls hurried to the quarry. They had time for a quick dip before the swimming race started, and feeling cool and refreshed, perched on a large rock in the shade to watch.

All of the boys were excellent swimmers, but Ben, in spite of his clowning, won with apparently no effort at all. "Nothing to it," he grinned as he joined the girls on the rock. "Before you stands the world's greatest swimmer. I shouldn't have entered an amateur race. It was like taking candy from a baby. As you no doubt noted, Sid here, was outclassed from the beginning."

Sid had been such a close second that everyone laughed, and Ben pretended to sulk. Sid hoisted himself up on the rock beside Trixie. "I'll bet you could beat boastful Ben with your arm in a sling," he said.

Trixie shook her head. "I couldn't, but Honey could. She's marvelous."

Honey flushed. "I'm not at all."

Ben scrambled to his feet. "Dare you to challenge me. Double dare you." He pulled his cousin down to the starting point on the edge of the quarry.

"Ready, on your mark, get set, *go!*" Sid shouted and they were off.

Trixie had not really been sure that Honey could beat Ben, but she did, by a whole yard, and the quarry resounded with the boys' loud cheers. Red-faced and embarrassed, Honey let Ben help her out of the water and before she could get her balance, he pushed her in again. That was a signal for everybody to drag Ben into the quarry and duck him over and over again. At last it was over and Ben, spluttering good-naturedly, held up Honey's arm and gasped, "The winnah!"

The dinner bell rang, and they raced away to change into dry clothes. Honey and Trixie sat on each side of Mr. Ditmar at the long table in the ranch house and had several helpings of the hunter's stew.

"Maybe you proved girls are the best swimmers," Ben teased, "but it looks as though boys are the best cooks."

"I won't argue that point," Trixie admitted with a laugh as she passed her plate for more of the savory meat and vegetables. "But I *would* like to know how you did it. Most stews are awful."

"First you take an onion," Ben said, his eyes twinkling, "and after that you weep and weep."

"Not if you peel it under water." Mrs. Ditmar smiled. "But Ben will never learn."

"By the way," Mr. Ditmar said to Trixie, "you're not the only people who've stopped at the ranch today asking for missing persons. A man came to the back door early this morning wanting to know if we'd seen his little girl."

Trixie stared across the table at Honey. "Was he driving a red trailer?" she asked.

Mr. Ditmar looked surprised. "Why, no," he said. "He was on foot and went off through the woods walking north. I took it for granted that he was a farmer."

Trixie laid down her fork. "Did he describe the girl?" she asked, trying not to sound excited. "Did he say her name was Joeanne?"

"No, he didn't." Mr. Ditmar shook his head. "He simply said she had black pigtails and was about eleven years old. I offered to send a group of boys through the woods to help search for her, but he rather rudely refused the offer and strode away hastily." He gave Trixie a sharp glance. "What made you think he would be in a red trailer? Do you suspect the man had anything to do with the recent theft that has been announced on the radio so many times?"

Before Trixie could think of a word to say, Honey interrupted with, "Did the man have long, shaggy hair?"

Mr. Ditmar laughed. "There's some mystery about all this, but you two are certainly on the wrong track. The man, and I think he must have been a neighbor farmer, had a closely cropped head—it was practically a crew haircut."

"Then I guess we're talking about two different people," Trixie said with relief. "We saw a shaggy-haired man driving a red trailer on our way up the river last week."

Honey quickly changed the subject. "You must come over and see our trailer before we go back," she said to Ben. "I'd like to ask you all to lunch but it's not quite big enough for that."

"I should hope not," Ben said as they left the dining hall. "It would have to be a young village on wheels to hold all of us."

Sid and Ben went off to saddle Prince and Peanuts while the girls said good-by and thanks to Mr. and Mrs. Ditmar. Then they rode off through the woods in what they thought was the right direction.

The minute they were alone Trixie said, "Didn't you

nearly die of excitement when Mr. Ditmar said a man had been asking about an eleven-year-old girl with pigtails?"

Honey nodded. "And I almost died of disappointment when he said the farmer had a crew cut."

"Well, *I* didn't," Trixie said. "I think Joeanne's father has simply had a haircut, that's all."

Honey, who had been leading the way, looked over her shoulder at Trixie. "I never thought about that," she admitted. "Then maybe the red trailer family is somewhere near here."

"That's right," Trixie said. "They've probably abandoned the *Robin* and are living in the woods."

"Oh, golly," Honey giggled. "You've got so many people hiding in the woods now it's a wonder we don't stumble over them."

Trixie grinned. "Maybe we'll do just that before we're through, but right now I wish we'd stumble across a trail that looks familiar. We should have come out on the field we galloped through on our way over to the ranch long ago."

"That's true," Honey said, frowning. "I never saw that brook before, did you?"

"Never," Trixie said. "Does it show on the map?"

The horses had stopped of their own accord and

were drinking thirstily. Honey produced the map from her pocket and handed it to Trixie.

"You figure this one out," she said with a laugh. "I got us to the ranch, now you get us back!"

Trixie stared at the map for a whole minute before she realized that she was holding it upside down. Even when she had righted it she was as baffled as ever. "I simply can't follow maps," she said ruefully. "Maybe we'd better go back to the ranch and start all over again."

"All right," Honey agreed, gathering up her reins. "But Ben will tease us for losing our way so quickly."

They rode along in silence for a while and then Trixie said, "Oh, for heaven's sake, Honey, here's the brook again. Now we *are* good and lost. I don't even know how to get to the ranch from here, do you?"

"No," Honey said. "But let's keep going anyway. Miss Trask said all the trails come out on a main high-way sooner or later. This path looks as though it was used more than the other ones. It's bound to lead some-where."

"Suits me," Trixie said. "I'd just as soon not go back through the woods. The deer flies are simply terrible."

The path grew wider and wider and finally they realized they were on a back country road.

"We're probably trespassing," Honey said. "I can hear a dog barking just ahead of us. I hope he doesn't rush out and bite us."

"Why, we're on somebody's farm," Trixie said with a gasp of surprise. "See the cows in the pasture over there? And look, Honey. Just beyond the pasture is that old orchard we saw from the top of the hill."

And then the sound of the barking dog came nearer. In a moment they saw a large collie racing through the fields toward them. Before the girls could gather their wits, Peanuts, terrified at the sight of the angry dog, bolted and set off up the road at a run. Trixie took up the slack in her reins too late. Prince was already galloping madly after Honey's big chestnut gelding.

Chapter 8
The Black Sentinel

A low branch slapped Trixie in the face as Prince raced up the road with the collie barking at his heels. Tears of pain filled her blue eyes and for a moment she was blinded. Clinging desperately to the saddle with her knees and pulling in the reins with all her might and main, she got out a few weak "Whoa's," and then she saw that Honey, a few yards ahead of her, had managed to halt Peanuts in front of a rambling white frame farmhouse.

Trixie sighed with relief. "Prince will stop when he catches up with Peanuts," she thought, bracing herself.

Prince was, in fact, already slowing from a dead run to a more sensible gait when a large black crow suddenly swooped down from a cherry tree beside the house. With a loud, defiant "Caw!" the crow flapped its widespread wings in Prince's startled face.

The horse shied violently and the next thing Trixie knew she was sprawling in the gravel driveway. The angry collie skidded to a stop beside her and stood there, growling threateningly, while the crow, from its perch in the tree, screamed insults down at her.

"If I lie perfectly still," Trixie decided in desperation, "the collie probably won't come any nearer, but I wouldn't trust that crow. He's as mad as a hornet and he could do a nice job on my face with his beak and claws."

And then she heard a woman's voice calling from the farmhouse, "Laddie, Laddie! Come right here to me, you naughty dog, frightening that poor little girl. Don't worry, child, he wouldn't hurt a flea. His bark is worse than his bite."

The collie, tail drooping, head lowered in shame, trotted obediently to his mistress. Trixie, keeping one eye cautiously on the bird in the tree, rolled to a sitting position.

An enormously fat woman with bright red cheeks and snapping black eyes was hurrying as fast as her weight would allow her down the back steps. "You poor lamb," she crooned breathlessly. "I saw the whole thing from the kitchen window. It was that crow's fault, the black pest." She shook a plump, dimpled fist up at the cherry tree. "Just wait till I get my hands on you, Jimmy. I'll make you into a pie so fast you'll never know what happened to you."

Jimmy Crow shifted back and forth on his perch as though rocking with laughter. Then with a hoarse, derisive "Caw!" he swooped down on an innocent little

garter snake that was wriggling through the grass under the cherry tree.

By this time his mistress had reached Trixie's side. "Are you all right, lamb?" she asked worriedly. "Such a tumble! You did a complete somersault in mid-air. It's a wonder you didn't break every bone in your body!"

Trixie laughed and scrambled to her feet. "I'm all right," she said, "but your pet crow had me scared for a while."

"My pet, indeed!" the fat woman sniffed. "It's my husband who has adopted the loudmouthed pest, and the pest has adopted me. He knows I don't like him so he follows me every step I take. I tell you it gets on my nerves, or at least it would if I were not so fat that I haven't any nerves." She laughed loudly at her own joke and patted Trixie's arm. "I'm Mrs. Nat Smith," she said, gasping for breath. "And you must come into the house and have some lemonade and cookies. If I do say so myself, I make the best chocolate oatmeal cookies in the county." She glanced down the road, her black eyes sparkling. "Your friend will be back as soon as she catches your horse, and then we'll have a nice tea party in my kitchen."

"We'd love it," Trixie said as she followed Mrs. Smith to the back steps. "But won't it be too much trouble?

I know how busy a farmer's wife must be all the time. We have a small farm farther down the river. Just a vegetable garden and about forty chickens, but it's an awful lot of work."

Mrs. Smith nodded as she began a slow, ponderous ascent of the steps. "Work, work, work from morning till night," she panted. "I tell Nat he's too old now to keep up that pace, but you can't stop him. And now with the beans all ready to be picked our hired hand fell out of a tree and broke his leg." She grunted in disgust as she heaved her bulk through the door and collapsed into a huge rocking chair beside the stove. "Wouldn't you know that good-for-nothing boy would pick a time like this to climb one of those half-dead trees down in the orchard?"

"Oh," Trixie asked, "does that old orchard belong to your property?"

"Indeed it does," the woman said, "although we haven't got an apple out of it for these past six years, and the boy knew as well as I do that it's not safe to climb those half-dead trees." Having regained her breath, Mrs. Smith shuffled to the refrigerator and produced a gallon jug of lemonade. She pointed to an enormous crock on the other side of the long, sunny kitchen. "Get out some cookies, will you, my dear? That copper tray on the wall behind you will do nicely. I'm not one for platters. They just don't hold enough. I always say if you're going to take the time to eat at all you might as well eat all you can hold."

Trixie heaped thick oatmeal cookies, dotted with chunks of chocolate, on the tray and brought it to the table while Mrs. Smith filled tall glasses with ice-cold lemonade. "These are the most delicious things I've ever tasted," Trixie said between munches and sips.

Mrs. Smith beamed. "That's what our hired hand used to say about everything I cooked. Poor boy! I'm sorry he had to go and hurt himself, and of course we're paying his hospital bills and his salary as well while his leg's in the cast, but I must say if he had to fall out of a tree he might have picked a time when we didn't need help so badly. All those beans!" She folded her hands in her snowy apron and rocked back and forth in despair.

"Why do you suppose he did such a foolish thing?" Trixie asked. "Even *I* have sense enough to stay out of a dying tree."

"That's the worst part of it," Mrs. Smith told her. "He gave as his reason that he thought he saw a tramp down in the field below the orchard. Now what would a tramp be doing down there? A tramp can smell as well as the next person, and even a blind one could find his way to my kitchen door and ask for food. But does that idiot boy figure that out? No, he climbs a rotten tree to get a better view of the field, and that's that!"

A tramp, Trixie thought. *Could it have been the bushy-haired man or Jeff?* Aloud she asked, "Is there an abandoned barn in the field below the orchard?"

Mrs. Smith glanced at her sharply. "A barn way off down there? Why would anyone build a barn so far away from the crops?"

"I just thought it might have been used to store apples in when the orchard was bearing fruit," Trixie said. "And a tramp might have been living in the barn."

Mrs. Smith rocked back and forth for a minute. "Well," she said, "if there is I never saw it, but of course, I haven't been able to walk that far since I began to put on weight about ten years ago, and we bought this place shortly after that." She leaned forward a little. "You'd never believe it, but once I was as slim as your honey-haired friend. This is the first time I've ever regretted my size. If it weren't for that, I'd be down there picking beans with Nat right now."

"Honey and I'll help pick them," Trixie cried impulsively.

"Now that's real sweet of you," Mrs. Smith said with a broad smile. "But you two young things couldn't stand the heat in that unprotected garden. There's not an ounce of shade except over the cucumber hills. And didn't I tell you that the good Lord, seeing our plight, sent us help last night?"

Trixie shook her head. "No, you didn't, but I'm glad you won't lose the bean crop."

Mrs. Smith crinkled her red face into a puzzled frown. "Now, I'm sure I told you when we came in not to slam the screen door for fear of waking the children who are upstairs taking their naps."

It was Trixie's turn now to look puzzled. "What children?"

"Why, the Darnells', of course," Mrs. Smith cried impatiently. "Three of the sweetest lambs you've ever seen, at least they will be when I feed them up. And, you know, my dear, I did tell you about the little boy's cold. That's why I had the lemonade all made. And I remember distinctly telling you how the little girl gobbled up my cookies."

Confused, Trixie wondered if she had perhaps received a bad blow on the head when Prince threw her, and was suffering from a momentary loss of memory. "I'm sorry," she began, but Mrs. Smith suddenly burst into gales of laughter.

"It's as Nat says," she got out between chuckles.

"I'm alone so much since the boys grew up and went away from home, that I talk to myself and then I accuse him of not listening even though he wasn't in the house at the time." She lumbered to her feet, her sharp black eyes snapping. "Here comes your honey-haired friend back with the horses. Just run out and help her tie them to that hitching post in front. Take off their bridles and let the poor things graze on the lawn. You'll find halters and rope hanging beside the back steps."

Trixie did as she was told. "Honey," she giggled, "thanks a lot for catching Prince, but let's not talk about that now. Mrs. Smith is the most wonderful person I ever knew although sometimes I don't know what she's talking about, but you never tasted such cookies and lemonade."

Honey stared at her as she slipped a halter over Peanuts's head. "Frankly, I don't know what *you're* talking about. Who is Mrs. Smith?"

"The farmer's wife," Trixie exploded. "She and her husband own this place and the abandoned orchard. Come on! You'll love her. She's almost the fattest woman I ever saw, but she has such a pretty face and is so kind-hearted!" Trixie pulled Honey along the driveway. There was no sign of the crow, but the collie, as friendly now as he had been angry before, trotted along beside them.

"Don't let that muddy animal inside my nice clean

kitchen," Mrs. Smith called from the other side of the screen door. But she made no protest when Laddie followed the girls inside and promptly curled up under the kitchen table as though he belonged there. "I declare," she said, "that dog is as spoiled as Jimmy Crow. I'll never forget the day Nat brought that pitiful little bird in to me. He had scarcely a feather—Jimmy, not Nat—and his long legs were too weak to hold up his round tummy. I was all for throwing him into the trash can but he croaked once as though he had the croup, and before I knew what I was doing I had wrapped him in flannel and was poking raw eggs into that big mouth of his." She handed Honey a glass of lemonade and waved a plump hand toward the mound of cookies on the copper tray. "Sit down and eat, lamb," she said. "You're as slim as Mrs. Darnell, the poor little thing."

"Oh, yes," Trixie reminded her. "You were going to tell me about the Darnells when Honey came back."

Mrs. Smith settled down in the rocker and it creaked protestingly under her weight. "That's right," she said. "And I may as well start at the beginning since Honey missed the first part. You see," she went on, "our hired hand broke his leg just when the beans were ready to be picked. That was yesterday afternoon. Nat sent for an ambulance and went in with the boy to be sure he would be as comfortable as possible at the hospital. While he was gone it rained so hard I thought the roof would cave in. I'm not one to be frightened easily, mind you, but I'm so used to having men around the place, what with seven sons until the youngest ran off last spring and got married, so you can see how relieved I was, Honey dear, when I looked through the window behind you and saw a man's face."

Honey shivered. "I would have been scared to death." She peered over her shoulder. "All alone in this big house, miles from everywhere and in the pouring rain!"

Mrs. Smith rocked with laughter. "Scared, lamb? Why should I be scared of a pitiful creature who looked like a half-drowned shaggy-haired dog."

Honey choked on a cooky crumb and Trixie's eyes popped open. A shaggy-haired man! She couldn't believe her ears.

"I asked him right in, of course," Mrs. Smith went on easily, "and gave him hot coffee and made him change into dry clothes. While I was warming hash in the oven he explained to me that he was traveling north with his wife and three children in a trailer, and wouldn't you know it, they went off the main highway and got stuck in the mud! Men, I always say, are forever taking short

113

cuts which never fail to take twice as long."

Trixie gave Honey a quick look. "Was he traveling in a red trailer?" she put in as Mrs. Smith stopped for breath.

"How should I know?" Mrs. Smith demanded. "When Nat came back from the hospital he dragged it out of the ditch with the tractor and put it in the barn." She chuckled. "I haven't walked as far as the barn since the dance we held there after young Nat's wedding and he has presented me with three grandchildren since then. But red or white it makes no difference. What is important is that Mr. Darnell borrowed the contraption so he could take his family with him while he looked for work on a farm upstate." She sighed with satisfaction. "It was the answer to our prayer, of course, and Nat hired Mr. Darnell on the spot. While they were discussing the bean crop, I got Mrs. Darnell and the children settled upstairs. Such a joy it was to have someone in those empty bedrooms after all these years, and the house filled with the sound of children's voices." She wiped her eyes with the corner of her apron. "I've been lonely for so long and bored with cooking for just Nat and the hired man, I don't know what I'll do if that family ever leaves me."

"Oh, I'm sure they'll never do that," Honey cried

sympathetically. "They must love being here."

"It's Mrs. Darnell who worries me," Mrs. Smith went on. "She's so frail-looking and yet she's down there picking beans with her husband. He's a grand worker, the best we ever had, and he and Nat will get the crop in all right without her help, although they did have to wait until the sun dried off the beans this morning on account of rust."

Trixie tried to gather her scattered thoughts. It must be the red trailer family, and if so, she should tell Mrs. Smith that Mr. Darnell had stolen the *Robin*. But somehow she couldn't do that. The Smiths needed help, the Darnells needed a home, and Mrs. Smith obviously loved having them here. *Anyway,* she quieted her conscience, *how can I be absolutely sure that Mr. Darnell is the same man we saw with the* Robin?

I have no business, she decided at last, *causing a lot of people unhappiness until I actually see that trailer or someone in the Darnell family.*

Mrs. Smith was rambling on between enormous bites of cookies and gulps of lemonade. "Such sickly little mites," she told Honey, who looked as though she were going to cry any minute. "I told Mrs. Darnell that I would take entire charge of them and fatten them up while she took a good long rest. But no. She insisted upon making the beds and washing the dishes and now she's down there in this broiling sun picking beans. I tell you, it worries me." Suddenly her broad face was wreathed in smiles. "One thing I did insist on, however, was cutting that poor man's hair. With seven sons I'm as good as any barber in the state, and the pitiful creature would have drowned in his own sweat if I hadn't taken shears and razor to him this morning." She turned to Trixie. "Would you believe it? That man is so devoted to his family and so short of cash, he hasn't spared the money for a haircut for two months!" She slapped the arms of the rocker resoundingly. "Said it would be like taking food out of his babies' mouths to go to a barber. I never heard the like, did you?"

Trixie, on the verge of tears herself now, nodded dumbly. *I don't care if he did steal that trailer,* she told herself. *Let the state troopers catch him. That's their business.*

Honey broke the silence with, "Why couldn't he get work in some other part of the state?"

Mrs. Smith's red face flamed with anger. "He had plenty of work until he hurt his eye in an accident and had to have an operation. Worked a successful farm down the river a way. But when he fell behind in his rent, the landlord threatened to evict him. Imagine it, with all those children!" Outraged, Mrs. Smith heaved herself to her feet. "And that reminds me, I must get those babies up for their juice and cod-liver oil."

"We must be starting home," Honey said quickly. "We've outstayed our welcome."

"We've had a lovely time," Trixie said. "And thanks for everything."

"Come again soon," Mrs. Smith called to them and waved from the back door.

The girls bridled their horses in a thoughtful silence and Honey held Prince's head while Trixie returned the halters and rope to the nail over the steps. Then she swung up on Prince's back and they trotted down the driveway to the main road.

"We're only about a mile from Autoville," Honey said. "I found that out when I went after Prince. The Smith farm is north and west of where the big routes converge. It seems funny to me that the state troopers haven't stopped there to ask about a stolen red trailer."

"It is funny," Trixie agreed. "Oh, Honey, do you think Mr. Darnell is Joeanne's father?"

Honey's hazel eyes widened. "Why, how could you think anything else, Trixie? He must be the same man with the crew cut who asked about her early this morning at Wilson Ranch."

Trixie sighed. "Well then, we've got to tell Mrs. Smith that Mr. Darnell stole that trailer, and we ought to notify the police too."

Honey squared her slim shoulders. "We won't do anything of the kind, Trixie Belden. That family has had enough trouble without our adding to it. If you set the police on him, they'll accuse him of all the other thefts. And I don't think he stole the trailer. You know perfectly well Mrs. Smith said he only borrowed the *Robin* until he could find a home for his family."

Honey was emphatically expressing Trixie's own innermost thoughts on the subject, so she did not argue. But she could not stop the pricking of her conscience. Kindhearted Mrs. Smith at least ought to be told that she was entertaining a thief in her home.

Unhappily Trixie walked her horse along the macadam road beside Honey. Deep down inside her she knew that she would have to return to the Smith farm the first thing in the morning.

Chapter 9
An Early Morning Call

As the girls turned into the entrance to the trailer camp, a uniformed attendant at the gate handed Honey a letter.

"Air mail from Canada," he said, "and horses aren't allowed here. Should I return 'em for you?"

Honey slipped off Peanuts's back. "Oh, that would be wonderful," she said gratefully. "We're terribly tired and I'm dying to open this envelope. It's from my mother."

The attendant grinned and led the horses away. "Hurry up and read it, Honey," Trixie begged even before she got out of the saddle, and said again as they strolled toward the *Swan,* "Hurry! I can't wait to hear what she says about Jim."

Honey read the letter.

Dear Honey,

Your father asked me to write you that he is seriously considering the matter of adopting Winthrop Frayne's son, Jim. I am not at all sure that it would be a good idea, but I thought you would like to know that we received your letter.

Miss Trask writes that you are very well and are having a good time.

Much love from us both, Mother.

Honey crumpled the letter into a tight ball. Tears welled up in her eyes. "That's that," she gulped. "I knew Mother would be against it."

Trixie patted her chum's shoulder. "Don't feel too disappointed, Honey," she begged. "We haven't even found Jim yet, and when we do and introduce him to your mother, maybe she'll feel differently about it."

Honey was crying in earnest now. "I don't think we *are* going to find him or Joeanne, and the next thing you know the police will arrest Mr. Darnell before he can return the *Robin* to that man who left it all hitched up and ready to go." She stopped and buried her face in the crook of her arm. "Oh, I wish we had never come on this trip. I never knew there were so many unhappy people in the world."

Trixie tried to comfort her but she felt so miserable herself she could hardly keep back her own tears.

All that evening after she had gone to bed, she tossed and turned, trying to make up her mind. *I can't turn that starving Darnell family over to the police,* she finally decided. *Anyway, not until I've made sure that their trailer is the* Robin.

It was still quite dark when she awoke in the morning after a troubled sleep. The sun was just beginning to paint the patches between the trees a reddish gold. Trixie dressed quietly and slipped out of the *Swan* without even disturbing the dogs.

"Honey is too unhappy already," she told herself aloud as she trudged along the road. "If I find out the Darnells' trailer is the *Robin,* I won't tell anybody but Mrs. Smith. I'll let her notify the police."

Birds were chirping in the trees and every now and then a truck whizzed past, but the rest of the world seemed to be sound asleep. Trixie knew that farmers arose with the chickens so she guessed that the Smith household would be at breakfast when she arrived.

She had walked hardly half a mile north of where the Autoville road came out on the main highway when she slowly realized that there was something familiar about the woods on her right. And then it dawned on her that she was standing only a few yards from where she had discovered the mysterious van's hiding place.

"Those bridle trails certainly do run around in circles." She chuckled as she gazed into the clearing.

"Honey and I had no idea we were so near home when we found that net."

There was no sign of the net now and the heap of evergreen branches had been torn down. "Honey and I didn't notice the clearing yesterday," Trixie muttered, "because on our way back from the Smiths' we were riding on the other side of the road. And Sunday afternoon we were so busy looking for bicycle tracks we didn't realize that the road to Pine Hollow is only a stone's throw north of the road to Autoville. Our only other excuse for being so dumb is that, after all, we were asleep when Miss Trask arrived at the trailer camp the night before, so neither of us had seen the entrance from the main road until yesterday."

She laughed to herself as she hurried on toward the Smith farm. "No wonder we kept getting lost. We never look where we're going."

If Miss Trask insisted upon driving home the next morning, Wednesday, Trixie knew that this was the last day in which they could look for Jim. She and Honey had planned to ride to Rushkill Farms after breakfast, so she must get back from the Smith place as soon as possible.

The sun had risen above the tall trees by now and although Trixie walked along the highway as fast as she could, she kept looking for bicycle tracks in the soft dirt in the shallow ditch between the road and the woods.

"I just know he's hiding around here somewhere," she kept encouraging herself. And then the sunlight gleamed on something that was shiny and metal on a rise of ground above the bushes on the other side of the road.

"Bicycle handlebars!" Trixie gasped and began to run in that direction. The underbrush hampered her every step, and brambles slapped her arms, but she kept on until the very denseness of the thicket forced her to stop. It was all too obvious that nobody could have dragged a bicycle through that part of the woods.

"I'll come back this afternoon with Honey," Trixie decided, "and see if we can find a path that leads to that shrub-covered mound."

Of course she couldn't be at all sure that the thing she had seen gleaming in the early morning sunlight had been part of a bicycle, but somehow she felt positive that it had something to do with Jim.

The air was hot and sultry now, and although the sun in the east was splashing the sky with rosy gold streaks, a heavy fog hung over the treetops of the western woods.

"It looks and feels like rain," Trixie told herself,

depressed again. "Oh, I hope the sun burns off that fog. If we can't look for Jim today, I'll die!"

And almost as depressing was the thought that they might never find Joeanne or discover the hiding place of the mysterious van. And, as Honey had said, Mr. Darnell might be arrested any minute for the theft of the red trailer. Then what would happen to his poor, half-starved family?

Hoping against hope that the Darnell trailer would not turn out to be the *Robin,* she trudged on, feeling like the worst tattletale in the world. It was awful to be torn between sympathy for the Darnells and her sense of duty. The only comforting thought was that kind-hearted Mrs. Smith might not notify the police, but would advise her new hired hand to turn himself in; then at least his punishment would be less severe. But in that case he might well be accused of the other trailer thefts, and how could he prove his innocence?

"Oh, golly," Trixie groaned aloud, "if only I had time to get proof that would lead to the arrest of Jeff and his bushy-haired friend!"

When she turned in the Smith driveway, Laddie came rushing out to meet her, barking so loudly that Trixie knew she could not now investigate the barn without being seen by somebody when she passed the house. Indeed, when she came nearer, she saw that Mrs. Smith herself was standing out on the back stoop with Jimmy Crow perched on one fat shoulder.

With a jolt of surprise, Trixie realized that Mrs. Smith had been crying. Her plump red cheeks were streaked with tears, and her black eyes were almost hidden in little puffy rolls of flesh. It would never have occurred to Trixie that anyone as cheerful as the farmer's wife would give way to weeping.

"Oh, you lamb," Mrs. Smith called, her voice choked with gasping sobs, "I'm so glad you came. Come right in and have some waffles and sausages and hot chocolate. I said to Nat only a few minutes ago, nothing will ever cheer me up but a young person around the place again."

Trixie tried to protest, but Mrs. Smith hustled her into a chair and poured batter into the double waffle iron, talking all the while.

"My precious babies' pictures, all of them gone! I wouldn't mind the locket so much, although Nat must have paid a pretty penny for it. Solid gold it was, studded with real pearls and turquoises. Of all the things they could have stolen in this big house, why did they have to take that?"

Trixie, completely baffled, rubbed her forehead.

"I'm awfully sorry, Mrs. Smith," she got out. "What happened?"

Mrs. Smith heaped sausages on a plate the size of a serving platter and pushed the butter crock and maple-sirup pitcher closer to Trixie. It was not until then that Trixie realized how hungry she was, and although she was dying to know what her hostess was talking about, she ate steadily throughout the conversation.

"It's my own fault, Nat says," Mrs. Smith went on between shuddering sighs of grief. "Although he's as bad as I am. Neither one of us can ever think evil of anyone. And that nice little Mrs. Darnell! Who in the world could have thought she was a thief?"

Trixie gulped guiltily and choked so hard on a bit of waffle Mrs. Smith had to pat her on the back. *Oh, dear,* she thought, *I should have warned Mrs. Smith yesterday. Now it's too late!*

"I took the locket out of its case to show Mrs. Darnell how my boys looked when they were her baby's age," Mrs. Smith continued when Trixie had stopped coughing. "It's an album locket, you see, and Nat had it especially made for me so I could have all seven of my lambs' pictures together; with Nat himself as a baby in the extra space. And now they're all gone." Mrs. Smith burst into tears and covered her face with her voluminous apron. She sobbed loudly for several minutes, her great shoulders heaving, while Trixie tried to guess what had happened.

"What makes you think Mrs. Darnell took the locket?" she asked when Mrs. Smith's sobs had subsided. "Have you accused her?"

"Accuse her?" Mrs. Smith demanded. "How can I accuse her when they sneaked out in the night and were gone without a trace when we woke up this morning?"

"Oh," Trixie gasped. "That's terrible. Whatever made them run away?"

"I don't know, I don't know," Mrs. Smith moaned. "And if they just stopped here to steal from us, why didn't they take the silver too and my teapot that's filled to the brim with my egg money?" She reached up on a shelf above the table and brought down a large pewter teapot that was literally crammed with bills and small change. "They both knew about this," she explained, "for they saw me put five dollars in it when Lalla Stern came over to pay her bill. The chickens are mine, you see. Nat gave them to me as a present and I pay for the feed and everything out of my egg money. I like to have a bit of cash that's my very own, and I told Mrs. Darnell that. And now, will you tell me why she took that locket and left all this loose cash?"

Trixie shook her head. "Maybe she didn't take it. Maybe you misplaced it."

Mrs. Smith placed her hands on her broad hips. "Do you think I look like the kind of woman who would misplace her babies' pictures? No, after I showed the locket to Mrs. Darnell I put it right back on top of the highboy in the parlor where I always keep it because that's where it catches the morning sun and looks so pretty gleaming against the shiny mahogany."

Trixie thought for a minute. Now was the time to tell Mrs. Smith what she should have told her yesterday—that the Darnell family had stolen their trailer. But was it necessary? "Have you notified the police?" she asked.

"I can't," Mrs. Smith wailed. "In spite of what they did to me, I can't bear to cause that poor family any more trouble. The frail little woman fainted yesterday after picking all those beans. And I think that's why they left. She felt she was too sickly to earn her bed and board, although I'm sure I didn't want her to do a thing but rest and get her strength back. I was fixing her a nice cup of hot tea when the little girl, Sally, came running in, chattering the way she always does.

" 'Oh, Mommy,' she said, 'Guess what! When I was taking my nap I looked out of the window and I saw

those girls riding away from here. You know, the ones that live in the big silver trailer with my black puppy.' And that," Mrs. Smith finished, "was when Mrs. Darnell fainted. She turned as white as my apron and pitched forward into my arms." Mrs. Smith glanced sharply at Trixie. "You never told me you knew the Darnells, but Sally insists that Honey has her puppy."

Trixie flushed. "We didn't know it was the same family," she explained. "We thought it *might* be the one we parked beside at a trailer camp farther down the river. That's why we asked you if their trailer was red, remember?"

Mrs. Smith rocked back and forth, pursing her lips thoughtfully. "I do remember now. And what's the story of the black puppy? Every time Sally mentions it her parents get very upset."

Trixie laughed. "Sally thinks all black puppies are hers because she had one once that died. She took Honey's dog with her when they left the camp and we didn't get him back until we caught up with them at a picnic ground." Trixie suddenly sobered. "Do you know what I think? I think Sally took your locket. She may have thought the babies' faces in it were her brother and sister. Baby pictures do look pretty much alike, you know."

"Impossible," Mrs. Smith declared. "She couldn't have reached up to the top of that highboy."

"She could have pushed something over and stood on it," Trixie argued.

Mrs. Smith smiled for the first time that morning. "You don't know my parlor. There's not a stick of furniture in it that a child of six could so much as budge. They're all massive mahogany pieces that belonged to Nat's parents." She heaved herself to her feet. "Come on. Look for yourself."

Trixie followed her hostess down a long hall to an enormous room that ran from one end of the house to the other. It was crowded with early Victorian furniture, and Trixie had to admit that she herself would have a hard time moving any of it.

Mrs. Smith slapped at a wasp. "I air the room every morning," she said, "and Nat hasn't put the screens up yet although I nag at him to do it all day long. I was telling Mrs. Darnell when I showed her the locket yesterday morning that now Nat had somebody to help him with the beans I hoped he'd have time to do some chores around the house." She sighed. "Such a grand worker that Darnell man was too. And I'd already grown to love the children. If only they'd stayed with us I would have cheerfully given Mrs. Darnell that locket, after I'd taken my lambs' pictures out, of course."

Trixie was staring through the glass doors of a ceiling-high corner cabinet. Some of the heavy antique silver on display looked as though it belonged in a museum. "Is this cabinet locked?" she asked.

"Heavens, no," Mrs. Smith told her. "Nat and I never lock up anything. And in spite of all the tramps I've fed and sent away again in warm clothing, we've never before had a single solitary thing stolen." She sank down on a tapestry-upholstered sofa. "I suppose I should notify the police, but somehow I keep hoping that family will come back. Mr. Darnell was very worried about that trailer. He only borrowed it until he could get steady work on a farm where his family could live. But he as good as promised Nat he wouldn't return it until the beans were in. Do you think they might have borrowed that locket and pawned it, planning to redeem it later? I mean, to cover their expenses while they returned the trailer?"

Maybe that is the answer, Trixie thought.

"If they 'borrowed' the trailer, why not a piece of jewelry too?" she wondered out loud and then bit her lip. She mustn't let Mrs. Smith guess now that the *Robin* had been stolen. Borrowing without permission amounted to practically the same thing as stealing. But if Mr.

Darnell, assured of a job and a home for his family, was returning the trailer to its rightful owner, shouldn't he be given a chance to correct his original mistake?

I can't give him away now, Trixie silenced her conscience. *On top of the locket's disappearance, even kind-hearted Mrs. Smith would feel she had to notify the police, and even if she didn't, Mr. Smith would never give Mr. Darnell his job back.*

Trixie looked up suddenly and realized that Mrs. Smith's sharp black eyes had been trying to read her mind. She felt her cheeks grow hot, and for a moment she was tempted to blurt out the whole story and leave the decision up to someone else. But before she could open her mouth Mrs. Smith said soothingly, "Now, now, dearie, you mustn't worry any more about my troubles. You've cheered me up so I think I can get through the day. I'll keep right on believing the Darnells just borrowed my album locket and that they'll bring it back soon."

"But what about the bean crop?" Trixie asked, anxious to change the subject. "Is Mr. Smith down in the garden trying to pick them all by himself?"

"Heavens, no," Mrs. Smith said as she led the way back to the kitchen. "They'd be covered with rust if anyone went near the vines until the sun has dried off the dew. Nat drove into the village just before you came to see if he could get some help there. But I doubt if he'll have any luck," she sighed. "People just don't like to pick beans, and I can't say that I blame them in all this heat." She fanned her red face with her apron. "I must get to my baking before it gets any hotter. You and your honey-haired friend come back for tea. Grape juice and chocolate layer cake. Spiced juice from my own grapes that I bottled myself last year. You must help us drink it up."

"We'd love to," Trixie said. "But I'm not sure we'll have time. We have to ride to Rushkill Farms and then—"

"Rushkill Farms!" Mrs. Smith interrupted. "Why that's much too far for you girls to ride in this heat. Oh, dearie me, if only I had a hired hand or could spare Nat, I'd send you over in the small truck. Whatever are you going to do at a boys' camp? You won't receive a hearty welcome, I can tell you right now. They're very strict about visitors. I ought to know. I drove over there once, when I could still wedge myself behind a steering wheel, looking for a lost calf. The man who runs the camp is about as disagreeable a creature as I ever had the misfortune to come across."

Trixie glanced at the clock over the stove and saw

that it was almost eight. "I've got to hurry," she said. "Honey's governess will be worried about me. I left a note saying I'd gone for a walk but I thought I'd be back before they woke up."

"Then run along, lamb," Mrs. Smith said. "And try to come back for tea. Nat and I can't eat that cake all by ourselves and tomorrow is my pie day. Every Wednesday I make lemon chiffon pie. Nat's mother always did and so I have to live up to her reputation." She chuckled, her own cheerful self again, as she waved good-by to Trixie.

Chapter 10
The Lookout

Trixie hurried down the highway to the Autoville road. She had stayed at the Smith farm much longer than she had expected to and was worried for fear Miss Trask would be cross over her long absence. Miss Trask seldom scolded, but nervous as she had grown since the trailer thefts, anxious to return it to the safety of the Wheelers' garage, she might feel annoyed that Trixie had added to her worries.

As she trudged along, Trixie tried to organize her jumbled thoughts. The Darnells had left suddenly in the night. An album locket was missing. But money and valuable silver had been left behind.

"I'll talk it all over with Honey," she decided out loud, "while we ride to Rushkill Farms. Mrs. Smith gets me so mixed up when she rambles on and on I just can't think. I'll let Honey try to figure it all out."

When she arrived at the *Swan,* she found everything in confusion. The dogs were racing in and out of the open door, daubs of boiled-over cereal covered the top of the stove, and flies were everywhere. But there was no sign of either Miss Trask or Honey.

Trixie stared about her in bewilderment. What could have happened to them? They had obviously left the trailer in a frightful hurry. Why?

Trixie shut the door and began swatting flies. Reddy and Bud promptly settled down in front of their empty bowls and looked at her hopefully with mournful eyes.

"Didn't anybody feed you?" she asked, opening a can of dog food and adding it to the scorched cereal. She stirred in some bacon fat and set the mixture in front of the hungry dogs. Then she put the empty cereal pan in the sink and filled it with cold water. Out of the corner of her eyes she noticed that somebody had knocked over a package of baking soda on the drainboard. "Baking soda," she said, puzzled. "What on earth were they doing with baking soda at this time of the morning? Not biscuits because I remember Miss Trask complaining last night that Regan had forgotten to buy flour."

And then she knew. A solution of baking soda and warm water was one of the best things to use on burns. Somebody had been burned. She stared at the scorched pan in the sink. Boiling cereal could cause one of the worst kind of burns. How had it happened and who had been hurt?

As though in answer to her inner questions, Honey called from the door, "Trixie! Trixie, are you back?"

Trixie hurried out of the galley. Behind Honey was Miss Trask holding her bandaged right hand against her chest. "I'm a clumsy idiot." She smiled. "Yanked the cover off that pot that sticks and knocked scalding cereal all over myself."

"It was a nasty burn and terribly painful," Honey added. "I made her go right over to the camp first-aid station."

Miss Trask's normally tanned face was quite pale, and she sat down on one of the bunks trying hard to disguise how much her hand hurt. "It's an ill wind," she said cheerfully, "that blows nobody good. The doctor said I couldn't possibly drive a car for a few days. So now you two have lots more time to look for Jim."

"Oh, Miss Trask," Trixie cried sympathetically. "I'm so sorry. You must lie down and rest and let us take care of you."

"Not at all," Miss Trask said briskly. "I'll be perfectly all right in a minute. You girls run along. It's a long ride to Rushkill Farms."

"We wouldn't think of leaving you," Honey insisted. "You can't do a thing—" She stopped as someone rapped on the trailer door.

138

Trixie opened it and a uniformed attendant handed her a yellow envelope. "Telegram for Miss Trask," he said. "We signed for it at the gate. Okay?" Trixie nodded.

"Open it, please," Miss Trask said. "And read it out loud. I haven't any secrets."

The telegram was from Honey's mother and Trixie read it slowly.

Returning home Thursday evening would like Honey there when we arrive.

"Oh dear," Trixie gasped. "This ruins everything. Your hand won't be well enough for you to drive back Thursday morning."

"Of course it will," Miss Trask said quickly. "I won't even know I burned it by then. I'm quite ambidextrous anyway and get along with my left hand almost as well as I can with my right. Run along, you two."

The girls cleaned up the trailer and left a lunch of salad and sandwiches and iced tea for Miss Trask. So it was after ten o'clock when they set off on Prince and Peanuts for the long ride to Rushkill Farms. They took both dogs so Miss Trask would not have to worry about them, but it was so hot they stayed close to the bridle path and showed no desire of running away.

The deer flies clustered on the horses' sweaty necks, and Trixie and Honey were kept busy brushing them off with evergreen branches. "This is awful," Trixie groaned, "and I know we're just wasting our time. We won't find Jim at Rushkill Farms. He's found out by now that he won't get a job at any camp without a reference. And Mrs. Smith says the man who runs the Rushkill place is an old cross patch."

"When did she tell you that?" Honey demanded. "So that's where you walked to this morning!"

Trixie then told Honey that the red trailer family had left in the night and that Mrs. Smith's album locket was missing. "I'm so confused now," she admitted, "that I can't make head nor tail out of anything. What are your ideas?"

"Why, it's very simple," Honey said, "although knowing Mrs. Smith I don't blame you for being confused. Don't you see, Trixie? The Darnells had to sneak away in the night after they heard that Sally had seen us. They must have heard the radio reports about the theft of the *Robin* and can guess that we must have heard them too. They couldn't risk leaving that trailer at the Smith farm another day after we visited the place. You said yourself yesterday that we ought to notify the police of our suspicions."

"I never thought about that," Trixie said. "And to be honest with you, I went back there this morning to see if the Darnell trailer *was* the *Robin.* I felt I ought to tell Mrs. Smith it had been stolen."

"So did I," Honey said quietly, "but I sort of think Mrs. Smith must have heard the broadcasts of the trailer thefts too. That woman is no fool for all her kindheartedness. My guess is that she liked the family and felt they deserved a break. As long as she never set eyes on their trailer she wouldn't have to face the fact that it was the missing *Robin.*"

"That sounds just like Mrs. Smith," Trixie cried. "And according to her, her husband is just as kindhearted. But what I don't see is, if Mr. Darnell ran away because he was afraid we would report him to the police, how did he dare stop at the Smith farm in the first place?"

"He had to take that risk," Honey explained. "He couldn't leave the trailer stuck in the mud. And actually it wasn't much of a risk then. The theft of the *Robin* probably didn't come over the air until late Sunday afternoon, and with all that rain there must have been so much static he could feel pretty sure people living out in the country wouldn't turn on their radios."

"And Mr. Smith," Trixie finished, "is so busy with those beans he probably never has time to listen to the radio."

Honey nodded. "And his wife is such a darling she probably *wouldn't* listen. Remember how mad she got when she told us the Darnells had been evicted from their home because they couldn't pay the rent?"

"What I can't understand," Trixie sighed, "is how that family could steal her babies' pictures after all her kindness. And if they did, why didn't they take along the silver and the money too?"

"It must be as Mrs. Smith said herself. They must be planning to borrow money on the locket for their train fare back to the farm after they return the *Robin.*" Honey suddenly straightened in the saddle. "Oh, Trixie," she gasped. "The poor things haven't got a chance. State troopers will catch them the minute they hit a main highway, and they can't stick to back roads forever."

Trixie uttered a groan of despair. "If only they had sense enough to abandon the *Robin* somewhere in the woods. Then when the troopers find it they'll think it was stolen by the gang that dismantled the other ones."

"Well, let's hope they do just that." Honey nudged Peanuts into a canter. "I know it's wrong of me to hope the Darnells don't get caught and punished, but I can't help it. It doesn't seem fair that I have so much money and they haven't got enough to live on."

"I know," Trixie agreed. "We're not rich but at least

we have a roof over our heads and plenty to eat."

They cantered along the trail with the dogs trotting behind them until they came to a large "No Trespassing" sign.

"This must be where the Rushkill property begins," Honey said. "And look on the other side of that field. A barbed-wire fence!"

"Maybe there's a gate," Trixie said, leading the way across the meadow.

But although they followed the fence for more than a mile, the only gate they saw was securely bolted. And then they heard a loud gruff voice and saw a man on a dusty gray horse riding toward them.

His light-brown, almost yellow eyes were expressionless, and he smiled coldly through thin lips. "Were you looking for someone?"

"Yes," Trixie said. "Is this the entrance to Rushkill Farms?"

"That's right. Didn't you see the 'No Trespassing' signs?" He twirled his crop impatiently.

Honey edged Peanuts closer to the fence and gave the man her warmest smile. "We would like very much to see the head of the camp," she said.

He gazed at her as though she were something on exhibit in a circus sideshow. "I am Mr. Snell. I am a very busy man. Kindly state your business as quickly as possible."

The sun was beating down hotly on Trixie's bare head. "We're looking for a redheaded boy who may have applied here for a job," she said.

Stiffly he turned from Honey to Trixie. "No one has applied here for a position since camp opened. Is that all?"

"Yes, thank you very much," Trixie replied with an edge of sarcasm in her voice.

He watched them impassively as they turned their horses' heads and rode away, and he was still watching when they cantered across the meadow and re-entered the woods.

"Thank goodness Jim didn't ask that old cross patch for a job," Trixie said. "That man would have smelled a rat and reported him to the police."

"Jim's awfully smart," Honey said. "I'll bet he took one look at Mr. Snell and decided he'd be better off working for Jonesy."

"So that's that," Trixie said. "Jim's been and gone. Our only hope is to find some trace of him at the spot where we saw the blue jeans. Let's return the horses right away. It's only a short walk from Autoville to the Pine Hollow road."

"All right," Honey agreed. "We can save time by

eating these sandwiches on the way." She handed one to Trixie and then gasped, "Oh, my golly! The dogs! Where have they disappeared?"

"Honestly," Trixie groaned. "This is too much! They tore across that meadow after a field mouse when we started following the fence, and that's the last time I saw them."

"We can't leave them. We're miles from home." Honey turned Peanuts around and Prince automatically followed.

"Wait a minute," Trixie cried. "Let's not go all the way back. There must be a fork off this trail that goes straight up the hill instead of around it. It's practically a young mountain. From the top we should be able to see the entire valley and catch sight of the dogs without searching for hours."

"You and your forks." Honey giggled. "We're sure to get lost again, but let's go."

Again they turned and, with Trixie in the lead, rode along until she held up her hand for a halt. "This looks like it might have been a path once. Let's try it; it's going in the right direction."

"That's about all I can say for it." Honey laughed. "Nobody bigger than a field mouse would consider it a path now."

Trixie twisted around in the saddle to grin back at Honey. "One good thing about it is that it's so tiny the deer flies haven't discovered it yet. Next time we go searching for missing heirs I'm going to take along a spray gun!" She turned around just in time to receive a smart slap in the face from an overhanging vine that twined itself around her neck and stayed there for several minutes. "Don't look now," she called back to Honey, "but the forest is following me!"

Honey laughed so hard at the sight of Trixie trying to extricate herself with the reins in one hand and a sandwich in the other, that she almost fell off her horse. But the path gradually widened as it grew steeper, and in the end it did lead to the crest of the hill.

As Trixie had said, the hill was really a small mountain, and they had an excellent view of the smaller hills and valleys below. To the east sprawled Rushkill Farms with its neat sloping garden and pasture lands. On the west they could see Autoville, a toy village. North of them, tucked between thickly wooded areas, lay the Smith farm. And, as an anticlimax, bounding up the steep trail toward them, were Reddy and Bud, tongues lolling.

"Let's ignore them," Trixie said grimly. "We're the ones who always get lost; they never do."

They started down the hill, taking another trail that looked as though it would take them straight to the trailer camp. But it didn't; it zigzagged in all directions, and by the time the girls arrived at the bottom they had no idea which was north and which was south. The dogs had left them long ago and they stared at each other in despair.

"Boy Scouts," Honey said forlornly, "lick their fingers and hold them up to the wind or something."

"There's no wind in the first place," Trixie muttered sourly, "and if there were how would we know in which direction it was blowing?"

Honey looked up at the thick canopy of evergreen branches overhead. "If we could only see the sun," she said thoughtfully. "It rises in the west and sets in the east, doesn't it?"

"No!" Trixie almost yelled. "It's the other way round. Besides, it must be just about midway between the two now, so that's no help."

"I suppose we could just give the horses their heads," Honey mumbled to herself. "They'd take us back to the academy eventually."

"I wouldn't trust them," Trixie sniffed. "They're so hot and tired I'll bet they'd head for the nearest stall which is probably at Rushkill Farms. All I need to finish me is one look at sour-faced Snell."

Honey, who was never as impatient as Trixie, smiled. "Remember the time you and Jim and I got lost in the woods near home? He said if we could see the river we'd be all right. He was going to climb a tree, but we were so far down in the valley—"

"Honey!" Trixie interrupted. "You're a genius. We're not in the valley now, this is a plateau. Here, hold my reins. I'll climb this black walnut. It's got the shortest trunk and the strongest-looking branches of any of the trees around here." As she shinnied up the trunk she said, "Wonder what a black walnut's doing in these woods. They're very valuable trees. We must be near or on private property."

At the first fork she stopped for breath, then climbed higher. At the third, she uttered a little scream. "Honey Wheeler, I don't know how we do it! We're on the very edge of the Smiths' abandoned orchard."

"What-at?" Honey demanded incredulously. "You mean if we had kept going instead of stopping we would have known where we were in a few seconds?"

Trixie grinned down at her. "That's right. We are too dumb to be allowed away from home without guides." Perched in the fork she went on, "I forgot to tell you that this morning on my way to the Smiths' I saw something shiny and metal gleaming in the sunlight on a rise of ground west of the main highway. I thought it might be the handlebars of Jim's bike because that mound is only a short distance from where we saw the blue jeans."

"Oh, Trixie!" Honey gasped, head thrown back. "You did investigate, didn't you?"

"I tried to," Trixie said ruefully. "But I just couldn't push my way through the thicket. But now I'm going to climb higher and see what I can see. Like the bear who went over the mountain," she finished with a chuckle.

Honey giggled and sang the old song as Trixie pulled herself farther up the old black walnut.

The other side of the mountain,
The other side of the mountain,
The other side of the moun—tain,
Was all that he could see!

She stopped with her mouth open as Trixie suddenly screamed, "Oh, oh, oh! Now I know who stole Mrs. Smith's album locket!"

Chapter 11
A Locket and a Barn

Honey craned her neck so hard it hurt. "Trixie," she got out, "you've climbed so high the rarefied air is making you dizzy. Come down from that lookout before you fall out!"

From the leafy branches high up in the tree, Trixie called back, "I'm in a crow's nest all right, and I do mean *crow!* In this fork is where Mrs. Smith's pet, Jimmy, hides his loot. So far I've counted two gold thimbles, three silver ones, a dollar bill, four quarters, several yards of tarnished Christmas ribbons, a brass key—" She started downward still chanting the list.

"—six marbles, enough bits of bright cloth to make a patchwork quilt, four silver spoons, a rusty razor blade, a ball of red yarn, and last but not least," she finished triumphantly as she slid to the ground, "one solid gold album locket studded with real pearls and turquoises."

She handed the lovely piece of jewelry to Honey. "See if all the baby pictures are intact. Thank goodness it hasn't rained since yesterday morning. That crow

probably flew out of the parlor window with the locket right after Mrs. Smith showed the pictures to Mrs. Darnell."

"Crow." Honey giggled as she released the clasp and unfolded the tiny sections. "He must be a magpie."

"A first cousin," Trixie told her as she mounted Prince, "and even closer to the raven. Jimmy's as bad as the one who perched on Edgar Allan Poe's door. 'If bird or devil,' " she quoted. "What comes next?"

"I don't know," Honey answered, gazing at the baby faces in the album locket. "Something about, 'Take thy beak from out my heart, and take thy form from off my door!' "

" 'Quoth the Raven, Nevermore!' " they shouted in unison.

"And that's no joke," Trixie continued soberly. "That crow could have caused a lot of innocent people an awful lot of trouble. Oh, aren't those babies cute? This one looks just like his mother. Let's take the locket back to Mrs. Smith right away, Honey. The farmhouse is only half a mile or so from where I saw that shiny piece of metal on the mound in the woods."

"Let's," Honey agreed, closing the locket and handing it to Trixie. "As a matter of fact, I'm starved. Those sandwiches we slapped together were awful. Didn't you say something about spiced grape juice and chocolate layer cake?"

"I did." Trixie licked her lips. "But let's be rude for once and eat and run. We might even have time to look for that abandoned barn before we explore the woods on the other side of the highway."

"Is there any reason why we can't look for it now?" Honey asked as they guided their horses between the rows of gnarled apple trees. "If this is the right orchard, it must be near here."

"I know," Trixie agreed, "but I think we ought to give Mrs. Smith her locket right away. She was terribly upset this morning, and that barn isn't going to be easy to find. It must be way down in a hollow and almost covered by the branches of trees. Otherwise we could have seen it from the top of that big hill."

"That's true," Honey admitted. "And we can't be sure this is the orchard Jeff and his bushy-haired friend were talking about. After all, if there is an abandoned barn near here, it seems to me Mrs. Smith would have known about it."

"Not necessarily," Trixie argued. "It's funny how you can miss seeing things on your own place. I'll bet you've never seen the old tenant house on your property."

Honey stared at her. "No. Is there one?"

Trixie grinned. "Mart and Brian and I found it one day when we were exploring. It's down in a hollow, too, and almost completely covered with wisteria and honeysuckle vines."

They were nearing the farmhouse now, and Laddie began to bark before he even caught sight of them. His bark was answered defiantly by Reddy and Bud who burst out of the wooded area just north of the orchard.

"Oh, golly," Honey gasped, "now we're in for a dog fight."

Laddie ignored the black puppy and challenged Reddy with a threatening growl. But the happy-go-lucky Irish setter, unaware that he was trespassing, immediately began to frolic invitingly around the collie. Laddie promptly gave in and the dogs raced off together, the best of friends.

"Reddy," Trixie chuckled with relief, "hasn't got sense enough to recognize an enemy when he sees one."

"Bud doesn't even know there is such a thing," Honey said, laughing. "Oh, there's Mrs. Smith at the kitchen window beckoning to us. I'll tie the horses while you take her the locket. I can't bear to keep the darling in suspense another minute."

"Neither can I," Trixie called over one shoulder as she raced up the back steps to the farmhouse. She let the screen door slam behind her with a loud bang and dangled the locket in front of Mrs. Smith's startled red face.

"Oh, dearie me," Mrs. Smith choked, collapsing into the huge rocker by the stove and hugging her babies' pictures to her wide bosom. "Where on earth did you find it, lamb?"

"In Jimmy Crow's nest," Trixie told her breathlessly. "High up in a black walnut tree. And here's the rest of his loot." She had tied the most valuable items in her handkerchief and now she spread them out on the kitchen table.

Rocking with laughter, Mrs. Smith kissed each one of her babies' faces and pinned the locket to the front of her flowered house dress. "This is where it stays from now on," she declared, "and at night it goes under my pillow. This time I make Jimmy Crow into a pie for sure." She sobered suddenly, her sharp eyes misty with tears. "And to think I suspected that poor little Darnell woman who wouldn't so much as borrow a straight pin she found in a crack of the floor without permission."

Trixie bit her lip. Should she tell Mrs. Smith now that the Darnells had borrowed the *Robin* without permission? Before she could make up her mind, Honey came into the kitchen, and Mrs. Smith immediately began to set the table for a feast.

"It's not the best cake I ever baked," she apologized although Trixie and Honey had never tasted anything like it. "Somehow my baking reflects my moods. I was so depressed this morning all four layers fell, and I couldn't do a thing with the icing. But this grape juice is the best in the county if I do say so myself."

The girls ate hungrily and drank several tall glasses of the delicious spiced juice. They were so busy eating and listening to Mrs. Smith ramble on and on that they didn't notice how dark it had suddenly become as storm clouds scudded across the sky.

"And to think," Mrs. Smith was saying, "I might have called in the police. Oh, dearie me, heaven be praised that I didn't. Nat would never have forgiven me. But he'll shoot that crow this very night or my name's not Mary Smith."

Trixie and Honey winked at each other. They knew very well Jimmy Crow would go right on stealing without so much as a scolding.

"That trailer," their hostess went on, "is the answer to their mysterious disappearance in the night. Poor Mr. Darnell is the nervous type. Afraid something might happen to borrowed property while it was in his possession. Although why anyone would want such a contraption is more than I can imagine. A house on wheels!

What will they think of next? I declare I'm glad our radio broke down so Nat can't make the loudmouthed thing screech all during supper. I'd be just as glad if something would happen to the telephone too. It rings all day and when I get to it it's always for somebody else on the party line, or whoever is calling us rings off before I can drag my body down that long hall. Such a nuisance."

Trixie, who was facing the window, saw lightning flicker in the sky and suddenly noticed how overcast it had become. If they wanted to look for traces of Jim, they couldn't afford the time now to go into a long explanation of the Darnells' stolen trailer. She pushed back her chair. "We've got to go, Mrs. Smith. It's going to pour any minute. Oh dear," she finished sympathetically, "that means your beans will get soaked. You'll never get them picked at this rate."

"Now don't you girls worry about me and my problems," she said. "Again the Lord has sent us help. Right after you left this morning, Trixie, two boys bicycled up the driveway looking for work. They're down in the garden now with Nat, and such a husky lad the big one is. Knows his way around a farm all right and will eat me out of house and home before the crop's in." She chuckled happily. "The younger brother is a puny little thing, but willing, I'll say that for him. Beans or no beans, I'm not going to let them leave this house until I've put a few pounds on Joe, that's all there is to it. If the Darnells come back after they return that trailer, all the better. We have plenty of room for them all, and I could use that little boy around the house, polishing the woodwork and doing up the dishes and such."

Trixie moved toward the door as a loud clap of thunder broke the outside stillness. "Well, I'm glad you'll save the beans, after all," she broke in when Mrs. Smith stopped for breath. "Thanks a lot for the wonderful tea."

"Come again soon," Mrs. Smith called to them from the back steps as Honey and Trixie hurriedly mounted their horses.

They waved good-by and trotted toward the main road.

"It's going to rain all the rest of the day," Honey moaned. "Now we can't look for Jim or the abandoned barn or anything."

"Yes, we can," Trixie said grimly. "We've got to, between showers. We'll wait at the riding academy until this storm blows over and start out again. It's the kind of a day when the sun shines half the time. See? It's struggling to come out from behind those clouds now."

Sure enough, it poured for about fifteen minutes

after the girls returned their horses, and then the rain stopped as abruptly as it had begun.

"It's awfully hot and muggy," Honey complained. "Let's not walk far. Can't we look for the barn tomorrow?"

"We can but we won't," Trixie said firmly. "I have a feeling that barn is not far from where we saw the bicycle tracks and the blue jeans."

"You must be crazy," Honey said wearily. "It's in exactly the opposite direction. At least the old orchard is."

Trixie shook her head. "While Mrs. Smith was going on and on about her new hired help I was trying to get my bearings, and now I've a nice little map in my mind."

Honey sniffed, but Trixie ignored her. "In the first place," she began, "we know that three big routes converge just north of the Smith farm. It stands to reason that one of them forms the northwest boundary line of the Smith property. It also stands to reason that since they sell their vegetables, there must be a road from the garden to that main highway. It would be silly to drag the stuff all the way out to this road when the garden is such a short distance from the other route."

"That makes sense," Honey admitted. "But what are you driving at?"

"It must have been the road from the main highway

159

to the garden that the Darnell family got stuck in during that rain on Sunday. They were probably riding along as carefree as could be, thinking that the man who owns the *Robin* was still away from home. Then the news came over the radio that he had returned unexpectedly and reported the theft to the police. What would you do in that case?" Trixie demanded.

"Get off the main roads as soon as possible," Honey said.

Trixie nodded. "That's just what they did, and the next thing they knew they were stuck in the mud on the Smith property."

"I follow you closely," Honey agreed, "but what's that got to do with the abandoned barn?"

"Follow me even more closely from now on," Trixie said and grinned. "Follow that road the Darnells got stuck on down to the old orchard. After it passes the vegetable garden, you probably wouldn't know it was a road since it may not have been used after those old apple trees stopped bearing six years ago."

"Oh," Honey gasped, "then that is the old road Jeff and his bushy-haired friend were talking about, and it must go right on down from the orchard to the abandoned barn."

"It has to," Trixie said, "since they were planning to

drive the van along it. It's a wonder the van didn't get stuck in the mud too, but heavy as it is, it must be much easier to manage than a trailer."

They had walked about half a mile through the fields by this time, and Honey interrupted suddenly with, "Where are you taking me? Trixie Belden, if we get lost again, I'll lie right down and die!"

"We should be almost there," Trixie said, laughing. "But first I want to ask you a question. If that old barn is so well hidden Mrs. Smith doesn't even know about it, how on earth did Jeff's foxy friend discover it?"

Honey looked at her blankly. "I give up without even trying," she admitted.

"Simple," Trixie said with a grin. "He must have seen it from the clearing where they hid the van before we happened upon it. The driver's seat is so high he could look right over the trees and down into the hollow."

"Then why," Honey demanded, "did they have to drive that van miles out of the way and through the Smith property to get to the barn?"

"Because," Trixie explained smugly, "there is no other way of getting to it except on foot. You couldn't drive even a light truck through these fields without getting stuck, and between the barn and the main highway are thick woods." She stopped and pointed straight ahead of her. "The way I figure it, the barn must be on the other side of that clump of trees."

They walked downhill for a few more minutes and then Honey sucked in her breath and let it out again in a long whistle. For only a short distance ahead of them, almost completely covered with heavy vines, was a high, dilapidated structure that looked as though a puff of wind would blow it down.

Trixie could hardly control her own excitement, but she quickly silenced Honey with a warning finger. "Sh-h, they might be in there now. Let's sneak up to it and peek through a window."

And then the rain began to come down again in torrents. Honey clutched Trixie's arm. "I'm scared," she whispered. "We'll get soaked if we stand here, but I wouldn't go inside that old barn for anything!"

"Wait a minute," Trixie whispered back. "I'll bet that old thing hasn't even got a door. I'll creep around and see if I can get a view of the front."

She crawled off through the trees, slipping and sloshing in the mud and in a couple of minutes she caught a glimpse of the entrance to the barn. One door had fallen off completely and the other hung precariously from a rusty hinge. There was no sign of the van or the men, but from this spot Trixie could plainly see heavy tire marks in the old road that led up from the hollow to the sloping orchard.

"Come on," she shouted to Honey. "The coast's clear," and raced for shelter.

Once inside, the girls stared around them in amazement. It was as though they had walked from the rainy outdoors into a storage warehouse. There were three almost new refrigerators with matching electric stoves, two radios, a portable Victrola, vacuum cleaners, lamps, mattresses and springs, pressure cookers, and all sorts of expensive-looking electrical appliances.

"Whew!" Trixie shouted. "There must be thousands of dollars' worth of stuff stacked around here."

Honey clapped her hand over Trixie's mouth. "Hush," she whispered. "Someone's coming! Can't you hear footsteps sloshing through the mud?"

Trixie listened and then grabbed Honey's arm. "Quick! Up in the loft." She started for the rickety ladder but Honey hung back.

"It'll never hold our weight," she gasped. "It'll collapse and we'll both be killed."

Desperate, Trixie gave her a little shake. "Whoever is coming is bound to be either Jeff or his foxy pal," she whispered hoarsely. "I'd rather risk the loft than be caught by either one of them."

Numb with fright, Honey began to climb with Trixie right behind her. They reached the top and crawled under the eaves just as the sound of men's voices came to them through the drumming of the rain on the ancient roof.

"—but what about that redheaded kid?" someone was asking. "Suppose he rats on us, Al?"

Cautiously Trixie bent forward and peered through a crack in the wide floor boards. Jeff and his bushy-haired friend were standing just inside the entrance.

The man called Al shrugged. "That kid doesn't worry me one little bit."

"I don't get it," Jeff whined. "Two dumb little girls scare you away from a swell hiding place right off the road, but you let that redheaded punk—"

"Oh, shut up," Al interrupted gruffly. "That kid isn't going to rat on anybody, see? Now, get the jack you so cleverly left in here. The van's not doing us any good sitting on the side of the road with a flat tire."

"I'm going to take a look up in that loft first," Jeff argued. "If he's hiding there, I'd like to have a few words with him."

Trixie didn't dare look at Honey. She held her breath and closed her eyes, listening with horror to the heavy footsteps on the floor below.

Chapter 12
A Fateful Sneeze

Trixie's fists were clenched into tight little white-knuckled knots as she waited tensely for Jeff to climb up the ladder to the loft.

And then Al's voice snarled. "You thickheaded numbskull! That kid's not in the loft. And if he is, so what? He's no more friendly with the troopers than we are. *Pick up that jack* and get going. Do you want someone to take a look inside of that van while you play hide-and-seek with a boy who's a fugitive from reform school?"

The heavy footsteps stopped, and Trixie opened her eyes. She peered down through the crack again.

The two men were glowering at each other. Jeff was not whining and cringing now although Al, a big, heavy-shouldered man, looked as though he were going to knock him down any minute. "You'd better watch who you call a numbskull around here," Jeff said evenly. "And in case you're interested, I'm getting fed up with your giving all the orders. This is a fifty-fifty racket, see?"

A sneer twisted Al's sharp features. "Fifty-fifty! That's what *you* think! I'm the brains of this outfit and I thought up the idea. I've also taken most of the risk. You're lucky I'm going to give you a third just to keep that big mouth of yours shut."

Dull red spots mottled Jeff's high cheekbones. "Why, you—" he sputtered. "You double-crossing rat! I've taken the big risk all along. Who forged those references so we could get jobs at the trailer camp? Do you think they'd have given you that classy uniform without those big-shot signatures I copied on the letters of recommendation?"

"That's just the point," Al said coolly. "You have a prison record; I haven't. All I have to do to get rid of you is to drop a small hint to the Autoville manager that it might be a good idea to have your fingerprints checked."

Jeff laughed. "You wouldn't dare. I'd sing a little song that would land you in stir so quick you'd never know what hit you." His expression slowly changed to one of deep suspicion. "So, you've been double-crossing me all along, huh? It was you who nabbed that red trailer all the radio ballyhoo is about. Got it hidden somewhere so you can make a quick getaway with all the loot sometime when I'm back there sweating in the kitchen." He took a threatening step toward the bushy-haired man. "Painted it a nice shiny blue by now, eh, with new license plates? All set to go, leaving me to take the rap when the cops close in and things get too hot, huh?"

"Don't be a complete fool," Al hissed. "Whoever stole the *Robin* ruined us and you know it! Since that happened there are more state troopers on the road than there are cars. As long as the other trailers were found right away, nobody kicked too much. Their owners were all heavily insured, so as long as they got their little traveling homes back, they were satisfied. But the amateur who made off with the *Robin* hasn't got brains enough to abandon the thing and give the troopers a rest." He whistled through his teeth in exasperation. "The sooner they catch that guy the better."

Trixie could tell from the frown on Jeff's ugly face that he still suspected Al. "No amateur swiped that red trailer," he growled. "Only a smart guy like you could pull one like that without being picked up before he changed into high gear."

Al reached into his pocket and produced a cigarette. He tapped it on his thumbnail and stuck it in one corner of his mouth without lighting it. Then he said, hardly moving his lips, "I've stood enough of your yap. As soon as you've changed that tire, we'll load up the van and I'll get going for the coast. I'll send you your share when I've sold the stuff. Or if you don't trust me, I'll give you a grand now and call it quits."

167

"A grand!" Jeff chuckled evilly. "Big boy, it'll cost you exactly five thousand dollars to get that tire changed."

For the first time since they had scrambled in fright to the old hayloft, Trixie stole a quick look at Honey. She was lying flat on the floor, peering intently through another crack. She didn't look the least bit frightened now; in fact it was obvious that she was thoroughly enjoying herself, as though she were safe in a theater watching an exciting moving picture.

Trixie smiled inwardly. Slowly but surely Honey was conquering her fear and timidity. When the girls had first met, Trixie had thought Honey was a sissy, but during the adventures connected with the old mansion, Honey had proved over and over again that she was anything but that.

She's a swell sport, Trixie thought, proud of her friend. *A couple of weeks ago she would have fainted dead away without even trying to climb up that rickety ladder.* And then she thought about Miss Trask. It was growing late. How long would the men stay down there arguing?

"You'll change that tire for nothing," Al was saying tensely. "If you don't, I'll beat you so your own mother will never recognize you." He clenched one big fist.

"We've wasted too much time already. That guy may come to any minute. The van's parked too close to his car to be healthy," he finished. "Whatever made you leave the jack in the barn?"

Jeff moved backward, cringing a little. "I didn't. Honest, Al. It was that redheaded kid, I tell you. If you'd only listened to me none of this would have happened. He took the jack out of the van and he loosened the valve core on that tire so we'd have a nice slow leak. Why didn't you let me tie him up and gag him when we found him asleep up in the loft last night?"

"Sure, sure," Al jeered, lighting a match to his cigarette finally. But he had lost some of his poise, for Trixie could see that his hand was shaking. "You tie him up and gag him and then what? He smothers to death and we have a nice little murder on our hands."

Jeff had apparently noticed Al's growing nervousness for he said quickly, "What about the guy you slugged and left in a closed car with the motor running? When he gets a lungful of carbon monoxide, he ain't going to be too healthy."

Al carelessly blew a series of smoke rings. "Ah, somebody'll find him before enough gas seeps up through the floor boards. I just want him to sleep nice and quietly until we can get the van down here. So will you please pick up that jack and get going?"

"What jack?" Jeff demanded sourly. "If you see one lying around you've got better eyes than I have. I tell you, that redheaded punk—"

Al lost control of himself then. "Stop yapping about that kid! It's getting on my nerves. He runs away from state reform school and stumbles on this old wreck. Sees a lot of trailer equipment lying around, but does that mean anything to him? How could it, blockhead? Unless he ran away with a walkie-talkie he doesn't know about our racket or that a red trailer is missing. Sure he sees the van, but what of it? This old barn isn't pretty but it's got a stone foundation and a good roof. Why doesn't the kid figure this is a legitimate moving and storage business we're in? That's what it says on the van. We charge cheap rates because we wait till we get a van full, then deliver the items all at once instead of making a lot of expensive trips up and down the river." He threw away his cigarette and ground it savagely under his heel. "I don't know why I tell you the spiel all over again. Thought you memorized it once so you'd know what to say if anyone stopped you on the road."

"You're the one who's wasting time now," Jeff said sarcastically. "You're the brains of the outfit and yet you let that kid get away after he hid up there last night listening to every word we said before we discovered him."

Al's narrow, too-close-together eyes glanced up at the loft, and Trixie's heart missed a beat. "He was sound asleep," he said, but he didn't sound sure of himself any more. "I can tell whether a kid's playing possum or not. And even if he did hear what we said, he's not going to run to the troopers. They'd clap him back in reform school before he began to sing."

"Reform school!" Jeff laughed hollowly. "If you'd ever spent any time in one of them places, you'd know better. Asleep or awake, whatever he was when we saw him stretched out up there, he ain't got the look. And punks who run away from the law don't carry silver cups and big heavy Bibles with them."

Trixie and Honey stared at each other. Honey formed the word, "Jim," with her lips and Trixie nodded. And then she saw not three feet from her face two impressions in the dust. One was oblong as though a heavy book had been placed there recently, and the christening mug would have fit exactly into the circular one beside it.

She pointed excitedly to the impressions, but Honey, grabbing her arm, was pointing in another direction. And Trixie saw with a thrill of pride that someone had tossed the missing jack into one of the empty stalls before which Al was standing. That someone had to be Jim!

Trixie felt like laughing and crying at once. Only the night before Jim had hidden in this very loft listening to the plans of two trailer thieves! He had not only managed to fool them by pretending to be sound asleep when they finally discovered him, but early that morning he must have taken the jack from the van and not long ago come back to loosen one of the tire valves so that the men's scheme would be ruined by a flat tire!

He really is the most wonderful boy in the world, she decided silently. *And the best part of it is that he can't be too far away now!*

The men were arguing in loud voices, and Trixie peered through the crack again.

"I can give you the story of that redheaded kid," Jeff was shouting. "He lives up there in that big white farmhouse. His old man gave him a licking on account of he played hooky from Sunday school. So he runs away and hides in this barn. A couple of nights away from home and he's had enough. So he goes back, but first he starts a nice slow leak on us and swipes our jack just for the heck of it. I can tell a farm boy when I see one."

Al's face turned pale. "He did look husky," he

admitted slowly. "And unless he lives around here, how would he have known about this barn? It was only sheer luck that I saw it myself when I was covering the top of the van with branches so it wouldn't be noticed from the road."

"That's what I keep trying to tell you," Jeff bellowed triumphantly.

"You fool!" Al hissed. "If you were smart enough to figure all that out why didn't you tell me before we got stuck in the woods right off the main highway two miles from a trailer we'd just dismantled?"

"You didn't give me a chance," Jeff snarled. "I wanted to tie him and gag him last night, remember? But I didn't think he'd pull no trick on us right away. I figure like you, maybe he doesn't guess we're not in a legit racket. I don't remember just what he heard us say last night."

He shifted his weight from one foot to the other. "I ain't too worried about the kid myself until we get that flat, and I open the van door and find the jack missing."

Suddenly Al, losing control of himself completely, hit him. Jeff staggered backward from the blow on his chin, and Al slapped him hard across one cheek. "You numbskull," he screamed. "I can tell you what he heard us say last night. He heard us say the hullabaloo over that missing red trailer was ruining our racket. People aren't careless any more. They don't park on side roads with their keys in the tow car and go off for a nice long swim. So we have to think of something else or quit. We decide to try the old hitchhiker gag. You heard the manager back at the cafeteria talking about a reservation for a salesman who's due to deliver a big luxury trailer to Autoville around noon. So I wait farther up the highway and thumb a ride from the driver. I show him a short cut and when we turn into the side road I tap him lightly on the head. Then you drive up alongside and we hitch the trailer to the van. We leave the man in the tow car on the side road and we take the trailer into the woods."

Al's voice had risen to an outraged bellow. "That's what the redheaded kid heard us say! Why didn't you tell me he looked like a farm kid? Don't you see, blockhead, he stole the jack this morning, then he came back a little while ago and fixed that tire so we'd frame ourselves nicely. The air leaked out just enough so we could hitch ourselves to the trailer and get into the woods a way, but there we are, just as the kid planned it, stuck to the evidence that will land us both in jail."

Jeff's face turned white between the red welts on one cheek. "Th-then you m-mean the tr-troopers are on their way here n-now?" he stuttered.

175

"Of course not," Al roared. "They would have been waiting for us when we came back for the jack if the kid had notified them. Like you say, the boy did it just for the heck of it, and now he's having a good laugh. Here we are with all this loot and no means of getting away with it. But the troopers have probably found the van by now, and sooner or later the redhead will lead them to this barn."

Jeff rubbed his reddened cheek dazedly. "I'm getting away now," he said slowly. "Loot or no loot."

"How far do you think you'll get?" Al sneered. "You with your prison record! If you don't show up when it's time for you to go on duty at the cafeteria, the troopers will put two and two together and get right on your trail. And that's just what I want them to do, except that I don't want them to find you until I've had a chance to board a plane and fly to the coast. If you take it on the lam now, they'll pick you up before dark, and then you'd squeal, you rat, and I wouldn't have a chance." He laughed and took a menacing step toward Jeff.

Jeff cowered against a stall door. "Wh-what are you going to do?"

"Tie you up and gag you, of course," Al said quietly. "And then I'll put you in the big oat bin. Nobody will think of looking in there when the kid gets around to showing the troopers our hide-out. And when they do find you, you won't have enough breath left to sing."

Jeff covered his face with his hands and burst into a loud wail that went on and on.

"Honey," Trixie gasped above the scream. "He'll smother! That Al is a terrible person. We've got to do something to stop him."

"Sh, sh," Honey cautioned. "As soon as Al leaves, we'll open the bin and then go for the troopers. I can't imagine why Jim didn't tell them to be here waiting for those thieves when they came back for the jack."

"I can," Trixie whispered back. "Jim couldn't go to the police station without being asked a lot of embarrassing questions about who he was and where he lived. The only thing he could do to stop those men was to fix that tire so the van would get stuck while it was hitched to the stolen trailer."

"I know," Honey argued. "But he could have telephoned."

"How could he?" Trixie demanded. "There aren't any phones in the woods. You know as well as I do now, Honey, Jim's hiding somewhere close by. He knew they planned to steal a trailer which was due to arrive at Autoville around noon. He had to time everything perfectly so he stole the jack and then waited until he saw Jeff coming across the fields from Autoville—the same way we came down here. Then he slipped into the barn and loosened the tire valve."

Honey frowned. "He took an awful chance. If those men hadn't got to accusing each other, they might have jacked up the van, changed the tire and got back here safely. As a matter of fact, in all this rain, I'll bet the troopers haven't discovered that stolen trailer yet. It's not like Jim to risk letting those men—" She stopped as Jeff, right in the middle of a shriek, suddenly lurched forward and catching Al off guard, tripped him.

In a minute both men were sprawling on the barn floor and clouds of dust floated up to the loft as they struggled and fought. They made so much noise thrashing about and cursing hoarsely that Trixie and Honey felt perfectly safe in creeping to the edge of the loft to get a better view of the battle. At last there could be no doubt that Al, the stronger of the two, was going to win. While the girls watched, fascinated, almost sorry for Jeff, he suddenly went limp with exhaustion.

In another moment Al was securely trussing him up with rope, muttering all the while, "This will hold you, my fine jailbird! I never had any intention of giving you a share of the loot. But now it's yours, all yours." He ripped a strip from a burlap bag and

178

crammed it into the unconscious Jeff's open mouth.

The clouds of dust created by the struggle made the air in the loft almost unbearable. *If I can't cough or clear my throat soon,* Trixie thought in an agony of suspense, *I'll choke to death.*

And then Honey sneezed. Frozen with fright to the edge of the loft, the girls stared downward as Al's bushy-haired head fell back and his fox-like face turned up to meet their terrified gaze.

Chapter 13
A Dire Threat

If it hadn't been such a tense moment, Trixie knew she would have burst into hysterical laughter for the expression on Al's face proved that he was as startled as though Honey's suppressed sneeze had been an atom bomb explosion. For one long minute he stared up at them, mouth gaping, and then a crafty look crept into his narrow eyes.

"So it's the rich little girls in the silver trailer," he said, quietly moving toward the rickety ladder. "Snooping again, eh? Well, well, well, we'll have to correct that bad habit. Nice young ladies don't snoop. I could use some ransom money to pay for my expensive trip." He placed one heavy foot on the first rung. "That governess of yours won't argue when I tell her to leave a fat roll of unmarked bills under a stone at the Autoville entrance tonight. She won't notify the police either." He reached up a grimy hand and touched one of Honey's shoulder-length curls. "Not when I send her a lock of your pretty hair with the note, eh?"

Honey shrank back as though she had been

slapped and Trixie thought wildly, *This is all my fault! I should never have exposed Honey to the danger of kidnaping. I should have come here alone. He wouldn't bother with me, I'm too poor.*

Out of the corner of one eye she saw that Honey was sick with terror, on the verge of fainting. All her life she had grown up with the fear of being kidnaped, and now it was happening. The sight of Honey's white, stricken face did something to Trixie. She sat up abruptly and, dangling her legs over the edge of the loft as though she were not the least bit frightened, said coolly, "If I were you, Mister Al, I'd get on that plane you were telling Jeff about just as soon as you can. I happen to know the state troopers are on their way over here right now."

Al chuckled and took another step up the ladder. "I always said you were smart," he told her. "Jeff kept saying you were nothing but a dumb little girl, but I knew better. You found our first hideaway, didn't you? But you're not smart enough to trick me into passing up a nice chunk of ransom money. If the state troopers knew about this hideaway, they would have been here long ago."

Trixie swung her legs nonchalantly. "Don't be too sure of that. That redheaded boy who let the air out of your tire is one of our best friends, and he's not dumb either. State troopers are like you and Jeff in one respect. They think kids are always playing cops and robbers." She leaned forward slightly. *"Unless* they have absolute proof that it's not a game. I should think," she finished airily, "that Jim has had just about enough time to lead them to your van and the stolen trailer. They must be on their way here now."

Fear flickered in Al's close-set eyes, but he moved up another rung. "Jim," he muttered sarcastically. "You made up that name. You never heard of that redheaded boy until an hour ago."

"Is that so?" Trixie fluffed up her short sandy hair. "In case you happened to glance at his christening mug, I can tell you the exact words inscribed upon it." She placed her hands upon her hips and swayed back and forth chanting, "James Winthrop Frayne the second. Right?"

She was so right that Al almost fell off the ladder, and Trixie chose that exact moment to help him on his way down. Raising both feet she kicked him on the chest with all her might. Caught off guard, he lurched backward, clutched madly at the top rung of the rickety ladder, and, still clutching the broken rung, toppled down to the floor below.

He lay there stunned for a second while Trixie wondered what she should do next to keep him from kidnaping Honey. Then he scrambled to his feet and shook the piece of splintered wood up at her.

"You're all part of a teen-age gang," he howled hysterically. "You and your friend and that redheaded kid and your so-called governess. Bet you stole that silver trailer and the red one too. Cutting in on my racket!"

Trixie felt too hysterical herself at this accusation to reply, and at that moment Honey came to the rescue. Trixie stared at her in amazement as Honey yelled down, "That's right. We stole the *Swan* and the *Robin* too. This is our territory, see? Scram out of it, big boy, or you'll get hurt."

Laughter at the sight of gentle, slender-faced Honey playing a hard-boiled part bubbled up in Trixie's throat, but she managed to hold it back. And now Al was slowly coming to his senses, realizing how ridiculous his accusation had been.

"Come on down, you two," he commanded gruffly. "I don't want to get rough but I'll count to ten. If you're not out of that loft by then I'll come and drag you down."

Trixie dug her fingernails into the palms of her hands. If only Jim could somehow have notified the troopers without risk to himself! She knew he had done the best he could, and as Honey had said, there was only a small chance that they might have found the stolen trailer and the van by now.

"—six, seven, eight—"

Trixie stood up hopelessly and helped Honey to her feet. "We've got to give in," she sighed. "He'll only hurt us if we don't."

"You bet I will," Al growled.

And then another man's voice cut in, "Put your hands up over your head and keep 'em that way!"

Trixie had just started climbing backward down the ladder, and the sudden command startled her so that she almost lost her balance. She twisted around in amazement and there in the entrance of the old barn stood two state troopers, guns leveled in their right hands.

"Reach for the ceiling, brother," one of them repeated as Al, still facing the ladder, stood frozen to the spot. Slowly Al's hands went up. "See if he's got a gun, Dave," the trooper said, "while I find out if the other one's still breathing."

He strode over to Jeff and took the gag out of his mouth while Dave patted Al's pockets. Jeff groaned as Trixie and Honey clambered swiftly down the ladder.

The troopers paid no attention to them, and Trixie couldn't think of a word to say. She felt as though she had been watching a moving picture and had suddenly become a very real part of it.

Dave produced a pair of handcuffs and said to Al, "Put your dainty wrists in these bracelets, bud. Pretty, aren't they?" He grinned at the other trooper. "Nice of him to tie up his friend for us, huh, Bill?"

Bill cut the rope around Jeff's ankles and motioned to him to get up. "One of them must have ratted on the other," he said thoughtfully. "Which one of you tipped us off that the trailer loot was in this old barn?"

Jeff and Al glared at each other suspiciously but said nothing.

"The way I figure it," Bill went on, "is that the big guy there was fixing to double-cross his friend. He knows he could never get out of the state with this stuff, but his pal puts up an argument, so he decides to frame him and gives us the tip about the hideaway."

"That doesn't make sense, Bill," Dave objected. "Why was he hanging around here waiting for us?"

"Well, then," Bill demanded impatiently, "who *did* telephone headquarters about half an hour ago? Any law-abiding citizen would have given us his name instead of hanging up on us." His eyes fell on the two girls then and he seemed to see them for the first time. "Say, what is this anyway, a quilting bee? What are you kids doing around here?"

Trixie thought quickly. *If I'm not careful they'll ask me about Jim,* she decided. Aloud she explained, "We came in here to get out of the rain and then that bushy-haired man tried to kidnap us."

The trooper stared at her suspiciously. "Was it one of you, by any chance, who reported to headquarters that if we looked in the woods north of the river road we'd find a stolen trailer hitched to a van with a flat tire?"

Both girls shook their heads vigorously.

"And at the same time," the trooper went on relentlessly, "did you suggest that a search of the abandoned barn below the orchard on the Smith truck farm might reveal the trailer gang's hideaway?"

"No, sir," Trixie and Honey said together.

"Well, I'd like to know who did," Bill exploded. "What was that you said about kidnaping?"

Trixie bit her lip. Now they were in for a lot more questions and sooner or later they would lead to the subject of a redheaded boy.

While she hesitated, Al innocently came to the rescue. "She was letting her imagination run away with her," he said shrewdly. "I'd rather kidnap a dozen wildcats barehanded than one of those two girls. The short one kicked me in the stomach and knocked me off the ladder."

Both the troopers howled with laughter, and in a moment Honey and Trixie joined in.

"You kids run along home now," Bill said. "We'll get to the bottom of this mystery at headquarters. Since we caught these two birds redhanded, we won't need to call you in as witnesses."

Trixie and Honey hurried out of the barn, relieved to avoid further questioning. It had stopped raining and as soon as it was safe to talk, Trixie said, "Why, it's not late at all. It seemed to me that we were hiding up in that loft for hours, but actually it was only a few minutes, I guess."

Honey nodded. "Let's go back to the trailer and see how Miss Trask is. Then we can explore the woods on the other side of the road."

As they trudged through the muddy fields, Trixie said, "I just can't get over those troopers arriving in the nick of time. Jim must have notified them after all."

"I was sure he'd do it, somehow," Honey said.

"Well, I wasn't," Trixie said. "When that awful Al climbed up the ladder, I was scared to death we'd both end up in that oat bin with Jeff."

"Scared?" Honey looked at her incredulously. "*I* almost fainted but you acted as though you were having the time of your life."

Trixie grinned. "I was shaking so I had to swing my legs so he couldn't see how my knees were knocking together. Then I thought it would be funny to swing my legs in his direction. It never occurred to me that I could knock him down off the ladder."

"You really should get the credit for catching those thieves," Honey said admiringly. "If you hadn't kept Al there talking he might have got away."

"You did all right yourself." Trixie grinned. "I thought I would die when you tried to act like a gangster."

"Well, that's one thing off our list." Honey sighed. "Thank goodness we don't have to look for a van or an old barn any more. Now if we could just find Jim and Joeanne, and if only the troopers would find the *Robin* abandoned somewhere in the woods, all our troubles would be over."

"Cheer up," Trixie said. "We know Jim's not far away, and I'll bet we find his hiding place this very afternoon."

"Why, what do you mean?" Honey demanded. "We found his hiding place. The loft in the old barn."

Trixie shook her head. "He may have hidden there one night, but he won't come back. That barn will be sealed as tight as a drum in a few minutes. All that stolen stuff is important evidence. Anyway, I keep having a feeling Jim is camping out in the woods somewhere."

Impatient to start searching, she raced ahead of Honey through the trailer park and yanked open the *Swan* door. Miss Trask was calmly reading a book and did not look as though she had worried about them at all.

"What luck?" she asked with a smile. "I guessed that you got caught in the rain and had to stay at Rushkill Farms until it was over. No word of Jim?"

"No," Trixie said and was surprised to see by the clock on the radio that it was only two-thirty. "We want to explore the woods some more. Can we do anything for you before we go?"

"I'm very comfortable, thanks," Miss Trask told her. "And my hand hardly hurts at all. I'm sure I can drive by day after tomorrow. I'm sorry Jim wasn't at any of the camps. Perhaps we ought to put through a long-distance call tonight to Mr. Rainsford. I think he should put private detectives on the case right away."

Honey, who had joined Trixie at the *Swan* entrance, pleaded, "Oh, no, let's wait one more day. If we haven't found Jim by tomorrow night we can call Mr. Rainsford."

"Very well," her governess agreed. "Run along then and have fun."

The girls hurried down the Autoville driveway to the main road.

"We saw those blue jeans about half a mile from here," Trixie said. "For some reason that trail to Pine Hollow Camp isn't shown on the map. The one we took from the academy wound all around the countryside."

"All bridle trails do that," Honey replied. "The idea is to get a lot of riding in, not to travel along the shortest distance between two points."

"It doesn't matter," Trixie said. "We've had a lot of fun, but now we can't waste any more time."

They trudged along in silence until they came to the spot where the tracks had ended at the macadam road.

"Why this isn't a bridle path at all," Honey gasped. "It's a back road leading to Pine Hollow Camp."

"I remember now," Trixie said thoughtfully. "We said at the time that nobody could have ridden a bike along the other trail. No wonder this road doesn't show on the map. It's probably only used by trucks bringing supplies to the camp. As a matter of fact, it's a private delivery driveway, I guess."

"That's the answer," Honey agreed as they started

up the rutted road. "Shall we cut through the woods or try to find a path?"

"Let's go around the bend and see if—" Trixie stopped as she caught a glimpse of the road beyond the bend. "Why, there's a car parked up ahead of us. Do you hear the motor running?"

"Uh-huh," Honey panted as she hurried behind Trixie. "It's gasping and choking as though it's almost out of gas."

Trixie rounded the bend first. "It's a sedan," she cried. "And all the windows are tightly shut. Who would close up his car and go off leaving the motor running?"

"Oh, Trixie," Honey gasped. "There's a man in there, slumped over the wheel!"

And then Trixie remembered something she had forgotten in the exciting events at the old barn. Something Jeff had said accusingly to Al, "What about the guy you slugged and left in a closed car with the motor running? When he gets a lungful of carbon monoxide, he ain't going to be too healthy."

Trixie was already tugging at one of the sedan's door handles, shouting directions to Honey. "Quick! Open up the other side. Break the glass with a stone if the door's locked. This is the man who owns the last trailer Jeff and Al stole!"

Chapter 14
Hair Ribbons and Pigtails

Trixie yanked open the door of the car and reached in to turn off the ignition. Frantically she tried to remember everything she knew about gas poisoning. If the victim had stopped breathing, she knew artificial respiration must be started at once. But how could she and Honey drag this unconscious man out from behind the wheel?

How long had he been shut up in that closed car with the motor running? Since noon? No, Al had said he only wanted the man to stay asleep until they could move the van to the barn. So he must have turned on the ignition and closed the car doors after they discovered the flat tire. How much deadly carbon monoxide had seeped up through the floor boards since then?

Trixie hesitated, and Honey, from the other side of the car, whispered, "Can you see his face, Trixie? Is it blue? Is he breathing?"

Just then the man raised his head a little and uttered a faint sigh. He looked pale and ill but in another moment he was sitting upright, staring dizzily around him and rubbing the back of his head. Gradually his color came back as fresh air circulated through the car. He looked at Trixie and then at Honey and managed a weak smile. "What happened? Where am I?"

"You're on a side road not far from Autoville," Trixie told him. "And thank goodness you're still alive. A perfectly awful man hit you on the head and stole your trailer. Then he came back and shut you up in the car with the motor running so you'd stay unconscious."

The man stared at her in amazement. "I remember now," he said after thinking for a minute. "I picked up a hitchhiker who said he knew a short cut to the trailer camp. I thought at the time that this road went in the wrong direction, but that's the last thing I remember."

"You were lucky," Honey put in. "I guess not very much of the exhaust gas leaked into the car. If it had, we might not have discovered you in time."

The man grinned, still dazed. "I don't know exactly what happened yet, but I seem to owe you thanks for saving my life. My name is Currier. I'm a trailer sales-man. I was delivering one to a Mr. Whitsun who was to meet me for lunch at Autoville." He glanced at his wrist watch. "Good heavens, it's nearly three. He'll be furious, and I may lose my job." He turned on the ignition. The motor caught, then sputtered and died.

"I'm afraid you're out of gas," Trixie said. "So we really didn't rescue you after all. The motor itself would have saved your life in the end."

Mr. Currier sighed. "I'm terribly confused, and the ringing sensation in my ears isn't making matters any better. Perhaps you'd better begin at the beginning."

"Surely you have heard about the trailer thefts," Trixie began.

"Why, yes." Mr. Currier nodded. "We've been warning our customers not to leave the main highways—" He stopped and clasped his forehead in his hands. "Oh, I see it now. I walked right into a trap. That hitchhiker was one of the gang!" He glanced behind him and saw for the first time that his trailer was gone. "But this is dreadful! They've taken Mr. Whitsun's trailer. He paid us eight thousand dollars for it, and it was completely equipped; even had a television set."

"Don't worry," Trixie interrupted hastily. "The troopers have found it already and captured the gang."

An expression of relief mixed with disbelief spread over Mr. Currier's pale face. "How do you know all this?"

"There were two men," Trixie explained. "They got jobs at Autoville with forged references. They stripped the stolen trailers of valuable equipment and hid it in an old barn not far from here. We were hiding in the barn when the troopers arrested the men about half an hour ago."

"Not so fast," Mr. Currier begged with a bewildered grin. "How do you know Mr. Whitsun's custom-built coach is safe? That's what worries me."

"Because," Honey put in, "a friend of ours let the air out of a tire on the thieves' van. It's still attached to your trailer and stuck in the woods near here. Unless the troopers have taken it away by now. After our friend fixed the van so it would have a flat, he notified the police where to look for it."

"Well, your friend is also my friend and deserves a fat reward which, I assure you, my firm will be very glad to give him." Mr. Currier started to get out of the car. "But right now I'd better give Mr. Whitsun an explanation of what happened. Is it a very long hike from here back to the trailer camp?"

"Only a stone's throw," Trixie told him. "And you can get gas there too, or send somebody from the garage for your car."

"I'll do that," Mr. Currier said with a smile, "I hope I see you two again so I can thank you properly." He waved and hurried down the road toward the main highway.

They watched him until he disappeared from sight. "I wouldn't be in Al's shoes," Trixie said, "when Mr. Currier tells the police how he shut him up in this car with the motor running."

"Neither would I," Honey agreed. "I guess both Al and Jeff will get long prison sentences."

"And it serves them right," Trixie said. "What worries me is that they'll tell the troopers about Jim and start them looking for him so he can be a witness. We've just got to find him right away."

"Oh, I don't think either Al or Jeff is going to talk about Jim," Honey objected. "Why should they? It'll only make matters worse for them if the troopers produce a witness who heard them planning to steal Mr. Currier's trailer."

Trixie shook her head. "Those troopers are dying to know who tipped them off. They'll make Al and Jeff talk eventually. Don't you see, even though they did catch those men in the barn it won't be easy to prove that they *are* the trailer thieves without Jim's testimony."

"What about Mr. Currier?" Honey demanded. "He can identify Al as the hitchhiker he picked up."

"I doubt it," Trixie argued. "Al must have worn some sort of disguise. Otherwise, Mr. Currier might have recognized him later when he was on duty at the trailer camp. He knew Mr. Currier was going to deliver the trailer to Mr. Whitsun at Autoville." She stopped and gave Honey a look of frank admiration. "You know, Honey, you're awfully smart. You figured out that when people stopped being careless with their trailers, the crooks would start hijacking. And that's just what they did."

Honey giggled. "I never thought they'd have the nerve to do it in broad daylight with the roads filled with troopers, and such a short distance from Autoville."

"They did have a lot of nerve," Trixie agreed, "and they would have got away with it, if it hadn't been for Jim. Oh, I wish he'd just loosened that tire valve and let it go at that. I'm sure the troopers will start combing the woods for him tomorrow, and if he gets the least bit suspicious that they're on his trail, he'll disappear for good."

They had strolled along the road until they reached a spot where the underbrush was less dense than it was near the highway. "Let's cut through here." Trixie led the way through the wet vines, still worrying. "Jim is so honest he can't bear anything underhanded. I suppose he had to risk setting the troopers on his own tracks to make sure those crooks didn't get away."

"That's what I thought all along." Honey sighed.

"And now I'm scared to death he may have already left this part of the state for good."

As they picked their way along, the thicket thinned out and became quite a respectable path. "Looks as though someone has been dragging something heavy through here," Honey said thoughtfully. "Whatever it was has laid the underbrush almost flat."

"How about a bike?" Trixie said over her shoulder. "Jim's smart. He'd be careful not to leave any signs close to the road, but this far away he'd feel it was safe to make a path to his hide-out."

"Oh, oh," Honey interrupted with an excited scream. "Look down there where the woods are thick. There's something stuck to a branch of one of those white birches. Something blue!"

Almost tumbling over each other in their haste, the girls raced downhill. And sure enough, caught on a twig not three yards from where they had seen blue-jean clad legs disappear into the woods on Sunday, was a dilapidated bit of frayed blue sateen. Faded and water-soaked as it was, both girls recognized it at once.

"Joeanne!" they cried in unison. "It's one of her hair ribbons."

"Then," Trixie finished breathlessly, "it was she we saw, not Jim. I'm almost disappointed."

"Well, I'm not," kindhearted Honey exploded. "I've worried myself sick over Joeanne. She's nothing but a little girl, and after all, Jim's perfectly able to take care of himself wherever he goes."

Trixie looked embarrassed. "I know," she said shamefacedly, "and I've worried about Joeanne too. But I did so hope we'd find Jim's hideaway before it was too late."

"Maybe we will," Honey said cheerfully. "The bicycle tracks ended near here. We have no reason to think Joeanne has a bike, but we *know* Jim has one."

"Come on," Trixie yelled, starting up the hill again. "Let's follow that little path and see where it leads."

It was hard work walking up the slippery, sloping ground, and they almost missed the path. And they *might* have missed it if Trixie's sharp eyes hadn't suddenly seen in the mud between the trodden-down vines and thick grass, distinct marks of bicycle tire treads.

"Now we really are on Jim's trail at last," she gasped, hurrying ahead of Honey.

The trail went on through the underbrush and into the woods where a heavy carpet of old pine needles hid all traces of bicycle tires.

At that moment Reddy and Bud, their coats muddy and matted with burrs, joined them.

"You tramps!" Trixie scolded. "They've gone completely wild in the last few days, Honey. We really shouldn't let them roam the countryside like this. They're sure to get into trouble sooner or later."

After joyful greetings, the dogs trotted off through the trees and then waited, as though they wanted the girls to follow them.

"Maybe they've discovered something," Honey suggested.

"We might as well go that way as any other," Trixie agreed.

They trudged along the pine needle carpet under the thick canopy of evergreens and suddenly came out upon a clearing.

"We've found it!" Trixie shouted at the top of her lungs. "It's Jim's camp."

There could be no doubt that somebody had been, or still was, camping out on the spot, for a crude canvas tent had been stretched between two trees on the edge of the clearing. Nearby were the ashes of a small fire between two upright forked sticks.

"That's just like the outdoor spit Jim built up at the mansion," Honey said. "He ran a pointed stick through a piece of meat then hung it over the fire between two forked sticks and kept turning it until it was done."

201

"I'll bet he built that tent too," Trixie cried. "It's even got a mosquito net. Let's peek inside."

They started across the clearing and then stopped as they both saw something that had obviously been ground into the mud and had been washed to the surface by the recent heavy rain. It was another faded blue hair ribbon.

Trixie stared at Honey as she handed her the stained bit of frayed sateen. "Joeanne again! But she couldn't have put up that tent. It took a strong boy to handle that heavy canvas. Only Jim could have done it all by himself."

"Maybe he wasn't alone," Honey put in quietly.

Trixie gasped. "Oh, my goodness. That's the answer, of course. He and Joeanne have met each other!"

"That's what I think," Honey said. "And it's like Jim to have let her live in this nice tent while he looked for some other shelter. I'll bet that's how he happened to find the old barn."

"He caught a glimpse of it from that mound where I saw something metal shining in the sunlight," Trixie went on excitedly. "That little hill can't be far away from here."

"Let's try to figure out what happened," Honey said. "We can only guess, of course, but this is what *probably* happened. It was Joeanne we saw Sunday on our way back from Pine Hollow. Shortly after that she met Jim or discovered him here in this camp. He gave her a nice supper and let her spend the night in his tent while he moved to the old barn."

"And that was the very night," Trixie added, "that the trailer thieves changed their hideaway. Jim heard them coming and hid in the loft and watched them unload the van."

"He probably suspected something dishonest was going on," Honey continued, "but couldn't be sure. So he stayed there again last night and heard them planning to hijack Mr. Currier's trailer."

"We know the rest of it," Trixie finished, "except where he and Joeanne are now. Let's see if there are any clues inside the tent."

They unhooked the mosquito-netting flap and ducked under it. An army blanket was folded at the foot of a bed of neatly arranged balsam boughs in one corner and in the other were stacks of canned goods— tomato juice, evaporated milk, corn beef hash, soups, and other groceries. On top of the cans was a complete Boy Scout kit of cooking utensils.

"Jim bought all this stuff a little at a time," Honey said, "at different towns on his way up the river. He may even have bought a secondhand bike in Sleepyside when he left early Thursday morning."

"Do you think he's gone away and left it all for Joeanne?" Trixie asked thoughtfully.

"Somehow, I don't think so," Honey replied. "Joeanne is the one who mystifies me. Why did she run away and then turn around and follow her family upstate?"

Trixie shook her head. "That whole red trailer family baffles me. I wish I could remember where I'd seen the *Robin* before—if I really did."

At that moment Bud wriggled under the mosquito netting. Before Honey could stop him, he had playfully seized one corner of the army blanket in his mouth and dragged it half off the bed.

"Drop it, Bud, you bad puppy," Honey commanded, patting his muzzle as she slipped the blanket from between his sharp little teeth. "Honestly, you're the worst pest—"

"Honey," Trixie interrupted. "Look under the boughs at the foot of the bed. Jim's cup and Bible and—oh, I can't bear it! Two long black pigtails."

Honey giggled nervously. "Joeanne has had a haircut too. But why?"

"I think I can guess," Trixie said. "After she lost her

ribbons she had an awful time keeping her hair neat. Especially in the woods where it would keep getting tangled in the brambles and bushes. Even if Jim bought her a comb, long hair would be an awful nuisance."

"It certainly *is,*" Honey agreed, shaking back her shoulder-length bob. "I wish mine was as short as yours."

Trixie grinned and snatched up a sharp knife from the cooking kit. "Just stand still, madam, and I'll hack it off for you."

"Not you." Honey laughed. "When I get around to it, I'll ask Mrs. Smith for a crew cut."

Trixie sobered. "It's getting late. Let's look for that mound. If we go uphill through the woods behind the tent we should come right out on top of it."

"I don't trust your sense of direction for one minute." Honey smiled. "But let's go. I hear the sound of a brook. That must be the one the dogs went swimming in on Sunday, remember? If we follow it we are bound to get somewhere."

They walked around to the back of the tent and then they saw the stream. "Let's not follow it," Trixie objected. "It runs down in that gully. Let's walk uphill. I won't be happy until I find out what was gleaming in the sunlight this morning."

With the dogs racing ahead of them they trudged along, and as they climbed, the trees thinned out until they realized they were halfway up a shrubby hill.

"For once I was right," Trixie panted. "Don't ever make fun of my sense of direction again."

"I'll believe you when we find a piece of shiny metal," Honey retorted with a laugh.

Trixie ignored her. "As the crow flies we are less than half a mile from the Smith farmhouse. We should be able to see it from the top."

"And that," Honey finished, "is the answer to your mystery of the mound. Do you see what I see dangling from the branch of that little tree just ahead of us?"

Trixie looked up and groaned. "Jimmy Crow again! Bicycle handlebars indeed! After this long climb all we find is another one of his treasures. A small, battered chrome towel rack." She turned around in disgust. "He can keep it for all I care. Let's go home before Miss Trask gets cross and worried."

Chapter 15
A Moonlight Search

The Autoville cafeteria that evening was humming with excitement. Everyone was talking about the capture of the trailer thieves, and the manager who had spent most of the day being questioned by the police, looked nervous.

"I never liked that Jeff," he told Miss Trask when she invited him to sit at their table and have a cup of coffee. "But he came to me highly recommended by an old friend I haven't seen in years. It never occurred to me to check either one of those men's references. The forged signatures were very convincing."

A man and woman were talking excitedly at the next table, and Trixie recognized them as the middle-aged couple Jeff had been listening to Sunday evening.

"I'm certainly glad you took my advice," the woman said with smug satisfaction. "If we'd gone off in the trailer yesterday, we might have been hijacked too."

The man nodded. "I had a feeling that waiter was listening to our plans when we were marking our route on the map at dinner Sunday." He shrugged. "I thought he was just one of those snoopy people who can't resist eavesdropping."

They left the dining-room then, and Trixie concentrated on what the manager was saying.

"I'd like to know who tipped the troopers off," he told Miss Trask. "I'd give the man a fat reward. I can't imagine why he had to be so mysterious about it all."

"Do they know it was a man?" Honey asked cautiously, and Trixie kicked her sharply under the table.

"Oh, yes," the manager said. "Those crooks made up a tall yarn about a redheaded boy who they claim was hiding in the Smiths' barn. Insisted he loosened the valve core on the van's tire and hid their jack. But the sergeant who received the telephone call said there could be no doubt that it was a man's voice. Quite a deep one, although it was obvious, he said, that the man was very nervous. At first, you know, they decided it was a fake tip-off made by someone with a warped sense of humor. They run into a lot of false clues, I guess. They almost ignored that call, and I can't say that I blame them. Why did the man hang up when they asked him for his name and address?"

"Did they trace the call?" Miss Trask asked.

The manager nodded. "Not until after they had

arrested Jeff and Al. It was made from a public phone booth in a gas station up the road a way. By the time the troopers checked it nobody could remember who had used the booth. Several cars had stopped there since noon, and neighboring farmers who haven't phones of their own often use that public booth."

Honey, ignoring Trixie's warning kick, asked in an elaborately casual voice, "Are the troopers looking for a redheaded boy? Some boys do have deep voices, you know."

Miss Trask, guessing that Honey hoped they would find some clue to Jim's whereabouts, glanced at her sharply.

The manager laughed. "Oh, no, the gas station attendants would have noticed a boy with red hair if he had used the booth. That was obviously a tall tale Al cooked up for some reason."

"Maybe Al himself made that call," Trixie put in. "He's the smart one of the two, isn't he? He must have realized even before the van got a flat tire that they didn't have a chance in the world of getting out of the state with the loot. He may have planned to frame Jeff but didn't get away in time."

The manager pushed back his chair and stood up. "One of the troopers seems to be thinking along those lines," he admitted. "But I can't see it myself. No, somebody who doesn't want his identity known notified the police. We probably never will find out who it was." He smiled and strode across the cafeteria to his office in the back.

"Has Jim got a deep voice?" Miss Trask promptly demanded.

"It's sort of husky," Honey said. "But I don't think it would sound like a grown man's over the telephone."

"I just thought," Miss Trask went on, "it seems like rather a coincidence that those men would make up a story about a redheaded boy hiding in a barn at the same time and in the same neighborhood where we're looking for Jim."

And then the girls told her that they were pretty sure that they were on Jim's trail at last. They even confessed that they had been hiding in the loft when the troopers arrested Al and Jeff. They carefully avoided mentioning that Al had threatened to kidnap Honey, but even then she was horrified.

"Gracious," she gasped, "you girls must be more careful. Promise me you won't go inside any abandoned barns or houses from now on."

"We won't," Honey assured her. "But the first thing tomorrow morning we want to explore the woods. If

we start out early enough we might even find Jim in his camp."

"Or Joeanne," Miss Trask said. "I wish I had known her father had gone off and abandoned her. I would have reported it to the troopers at once. What kind of a man would do such a thing? I've a good mind to notify the police right now."

"Oh, please don't," Honey begged. "He didn't really abandon her, Miss Trask. She ran away, and he had to think of his wife and the other children. As soon as he found a home for them I'm sure he meant to go back and look for Joeanne."

"Anyway," Trixie added, "Joeanne knew where her family was going." She clapped her hand over her mouth too late. She had not meant to let Miss Trask even guess that the stolen red trailer might be somewhere in the vicinity. If she knew that it had been parked in the Smith garage until the night before she would certainly feel that she should report it to the police.

Fortunately Miss Trask's suspicions were not aroused, and Honey quickly changed the subject. "We'll find Joeanne when we find Jim," she said so positively that even Trixie was impressed. "I'm not worried about her at all now that Jim's looking out for her."

She slipped her arm through Trixie's as they

followed the governess out of the cafeteria. Miss Trask stopped at the magazine stand, and the girls went down the steps to the park. "Listen," Honey whispered, "she wants to go to the outdoor movies tonight, but we'll say we're too tired, which is the absolute truth. Only, after a short rest, let's go back and see if we can find someone sleeping in that tent at Jim's camp. If we find Joeanne we'll make her tell us where Jim is."

"Wonderful," Trixie cried. "We can get there and be back long before the movie is over."

Honey nodded. "I wouldn't deceive Miss Trask for anything in the world, but you know perfectly well she would never give us permission to go into the woods at night. And it seems to me it's the one sure way of finding somebody at Jim's camp. After it's all over and we're back safely, she'll understand why we had to do it without telling her."

"I know," Trixie agreed. "She's an awfully good sport. I was terrified back at the table that she'd start the troopers looking for Joeanne."

"Miss Trask knows we want to find her when we find Jim," Honey went on. "But if we don't find one or both of them by tomorrow she'll *have* to notify Mr. Rainsford as well as the police."

"We've got to find one of them this evening," Trixie

said grimly. Then she chuckled. "You're always calling yourself a fraidy-cat but I notice you don't seem at all scared at the idea of going into the woods tonight."

Honey's hazel eyes widened in surprise. "Of course not! It'll be as light as day with that big moon shining. It's still almost as bright as it was last Wednesday when you and I and Jim went for a moonlight ride, remember?"

"I sure do," Trixie said. "And I haven't forgotten how Reddy kept delaying our start. Oh, golly," she interrupted herself. "That reminds me. Where are those dogs now?"

Miss Trask joined them as they stopped by the swimming pool. "You girls look tired," she said. "I'll run along to the movie and let you topple into bed. You must go to sleep early if you want to look for Jim the first thing tomorrow morning."

She smiled and hurried past them on her way to the parking lot.

"Those dogs," Honey groaned. "I can't remember now whether or not they were with us when we found Jimmy Crow's towel rack. Can you?"

Trixie thought for a minute. "Reddy was. I was so disappointed and turned around to go home so suddenly I almost tripped over him."

"That's right," Honey went on, "and I do remember

now. He was with us when we got back to the trailer. He barged by us when we opened the door and jumped up on the couch where Miss Trask was reading. She pushed him down and brushed off his muddy footprints. I just took it for granted that Bud was with us too."

They hurried to the *Swan* and sure enough, Reddy was there, looking bored and hungry. But there was no sign of the little black cocker spaniel puppy.

"We're perfectly awful, Honey," Trixie said as she opened a can of dog food. "We don't deserve to have pets if we can't take better care of them. The water in their pan hasn't been emptied and refilled for ages I'll bet."

"I did it this morning," Honey said quickly. "That's what I was doing when Miss Trask burned herself. Oh, dear, Trixie, where do you suppose Bud is?"

Trixie grinned suddenly. "At least, we have a good excuse now to go back to the woods across the road. He must be around there. Maybe his sense of direction is no better than ours. He's nothing but a puppy, so when he got tired of looking for us, he may have collapsed under a tree and gone to sleep."

"I hope so," Honey said as she followed Trixie out of the *Swan,* carefully shutting Reddy inside. "The first thing I'm going to do when we get back home is to teach that little wretch to heel."

Trixie laughed. "You'd better first train him to come when called. He's as bad as Reddy who only comes when he hasn't anything better to do."

"It seems to me," Honey complained as they hurried down the Autoville driveway, "that we never have less than three things to look for at the same time. Wouldn't it be heavenly if Bud met Jim in the woods and we found them both at the camp?"

"Bud doesn't know Jim," Trixie objected. "Reddy does, but you always shut Bud inside the house when we went up to the mansion."

"Bud knows Joeanne," Honey pointed out. "He spent a whole morning in the red trailer. Maybe he's asleep in the tent with her right now."

"It's too hot and too early for anyone to be asleep," Trixie said. "The movies started at eight so it's only a little after that now."

They walked along in silence until they came to the Pine Hollow road. As they rounded the bend they saw that Mr. Currier's automobile was no longer there, then they cut through the woods.

With the aid of their flashlight and the bright moonlight, they easily followed the path, and in a short while they arrived at the little camp in the clearing. There was no sign of life and Bud did not appear in answer to their shouts and whistles.

"The ashes are cold," Trixie said, patting the remnants of the fire between the two forked sticks. "Nobody has been cooking here today."

Honey lifted the mosquito-net flap to the tent. "Everything is exactly as we left it," she sighed. "Even that wrinkle in the blanket I forgot to smooth out after Bud yanked it off the bed."

"Well, I'm going to leave a note for Jim," Trixie said, refusing to become depressed. "Sooner or later, he's bound to come back after his mug and Bible."

"But we haven't any paper or pencil," Honey said, looking as though she were going to cry.

"I'll tear a label off one of the cans," Trixie told her, "and write on the back of it with a hunk of charred wood from the dead fire."

"You're wonderful," Honey cried, cheering up as she slipped out of the tent and hurried back with a piece of charcoal. "What are you going to say?"

Trixie thought for a minute and then she wrote.

Jim: Honey and I are at the Autoville trailer camp. It is perfectly safe now for you to come to see us. Trixie.

"There isn't room for another word," she said, "but he trusts us so he'll come. I'll stick the note inside his christening mug so he can't possibly miss seeing it."

"Now what'll we do about Bud?" Honey demanded as they replaced the corner of the blanket over the foot of the bed and scrambled out of the tent.

"We could climb up to the top of that shrubby hill," Trixie suggested, "but I doubt if we could catch a glimpse of him from there, not in the moonlight."

"Oh dear," Honey moaned. "I can't bear to think of the poor little thing spending a night alone in the woods."

"It won't hurt him at all," Trixie declared emphatically. "It's very warm and there's plenty of water for him to drink. He may even have caught a small field mouse for his supper."

"I suppose the sensible thing for us to do is go home and look for Bud again early in the morning," Honey said after they had called and called in vain.

"That's right," Trixie agreed. "I'm so tired I don't think I could climb that hill and that's probably where he is. Both dogs were with us when the trees thinned out and began to be shrubs. That's the last time I remember seeing Bud. He raced ahead of us but Reddy stayed close by for a wonder." She yawned wearily.

"I'm exhausted too," Honey admitted. "Let's give up."

On the way home Trixie suddenly thought of something, but she decided not to say anything to

Honey for fear of arousing false hopes.

What Trixie thought of was a little barefoot girl in a patched sunsuit, cradling a black puppy to her thin body. "My puppy," Sally had crooned the day they had first met the red trailer family.

Did Bud's disappearance mean that the stolen *Robin* was hidden somewhere nearby?

"If it is," Trixie whispered to herself as she curled up in bed, "we should be able to see it from the top of that shrub-covered rise of land. Maybe Jimmy Crow has done us a favor after all. If it hadn't been for his shiny towel rack, I would never have noticed that mound."

Chapter 16
A Surprising Slide

The girls slept soundly until dawn. They ate a hurried breakfast of dry cereal and milk and left the *Swan*.

The sun had not yet burned off the dew, and there were still mud puddles in the Autoville driveway, left over from yesterday's rain. A heavy mist blotted out the treetops but Trixie felt sure that before noon the sky would be clear and bright. She was also sure, with a growing sense of excitement, that before the day was over they would find not only Jim and Joeanne, but the red trailer family as well.

Joeanne might well have spent the night in the *Robin* with her parents. She told herself that was why Joeanne wasn't in the tent at Jim's camp. She had probably discovered the trailer in the woods somewhere yesterday.

"I had the funniest dream last night," Honey said as they left the Pine Hollow road and cut through the woods toward the little camp in the clearing. "And it was all in color like a Technicolor movie."

Trixie grinned. "Only people with very vivid imaginations dream in color. You'll probably be a writer or an artist someday, Honey. What was the dream about?"

"It was just as plain as could be," Honey told her. "Bud had grown to an enormous size and he was hitched up to the red trailer. I was riding on his back and you and Jim were running alongside. Jim's hair was as red as the sunrise, and then suddenly it turned as black as night and I saw it wasn't Jim, but Joeanne. She ran along with her hair flowing behind her like a black cloud, screaming, 'Nevermore, nevermore,' and sobbing heartbrokenly. All of a sudden she changed into a large black raven and flew away, flapping her wings and croaking."

Trixie giggled. "What happened to me? Did I change into a pumpkin or something?"

"No." Honey smiled. "You stayed just the way you are, and it was perfectly maddening. I kept yelling at you, 'Catch her! Catch her!' but you just grinned at me like the Cheshire cat in 'Through the Looking Glass.' "

"Like this?" Trixie screwed her face into an evil grin.

Honey nodded soberly. "I know this sounds crazy, but that nightmare makes sense in a way. I mean," she hurried on as Trixie stared at her, "about Joeanne. I've been thinking about her ever since I woke up and how she cried 'Nevermore' in the dream. Don't you see? What she was really sobbing was, 'Never again. Never again.' "

"Why, Honey Wheeler," Trixie gasped, "you're positively a wizard! I get it now. Joeanne ran away but she was sorry right afterward, so she started out to look for her family. She must have known her father was going to try to get work on one of the big truck farms around here, and *he* knew that *she* knew it, so that's why he didn't worry about her too much. He was sure she'd show up sooner or later in this farming district."

"That's the way I figure it," Honey said slowly. "Except that I think her family worried an awful lot about her but couldn't do anything."

"I'll bet her father felt it served her right," Trixie said, "and that spending a night in the woods would teach her a good lesson. I ran away from home once," she went on with a rueful giggle, "when I was just about Joeanne's age. I hid in the woods between your place and ours and waited for them to come and find me with bloodhounds and mounted policemen. I had a wonderful time thinking how sad they were going to be when they found me starved to death under a tree, and I kept watching the house for signs of excitement. But nothing happened at all. Everybody went on about his business just as though nobody had even missed me. They had a lovely picnic supper out on the terrace, and I almost gave up when I saw they were having vanilla ice cream with hot fudge sauce for dessert."

Honey burst into gales of laughter. "I bet that just about killed you! What finally happened?"

Trixie grinned. "Well, after supper, they calmly and coolly went to bed. One by one, the lights went out and it got darker and darker in the woods. I made up my mind I was going to stick it out but just then a huge owl swooped down so close I could have touched its wings, hooting, 'Who-who, whooo!' and that finished me. I scampered for home, bawling like a baby."

"Did you get an awful scolding?" Honey asked.

Trixie shook her head. "Nobody said a word, not even Bobby. Dad let me in the back door just as though it was perfectly normal for me to be out until ten o'clock, and I went right upstairs to bed without even asking for something to eat although I was ravenous. I can tell you," she finished, "I've never had any desire to run away since, and I'll bet Joeanne has learned her lesson too."

"I guess she has," Honey agreed, "but all the same, I'm glad Jim has been looking out for her. The poor little thing, all alone in the woods without anything to eat and in all that rain!"

"I know," Trixie admitted, "but she didn't *have* to stay in the woods. Any of the farmers around here would have taken her in. Farmers are usually kind and hospitable, like Mrs. Smith."

"How do you suppose she got all the way up here from that picnic ground?" Honey wondered out loud. "She couldn't have walked that far between Saturday afternoon and Sunday morning."

"She hitchhiked, of course," Trixie said, "and probably arrived in this part of the river country at about the same time we did. Miss Trask drove at the rate of twenty miles an hour, but a car without a trailer would travel much faster."

"I wonder where she spent Saturday night," Honey wanted to know. "I'm glad it didn't rain, aren't you?"

Trixie nodded. "And it was nice and hot. I remember thinking I was going to suffocate inside the *Swan*. It was probably a perfect night for sleeping outdoors, and you know yourself, Honey, eleven-year-old girls aren't exactly babies. We were that age only a couple of years ago. Joeanne seems pathetic to us because she's so thin, but remember how grownup and independent she acted that first evening when we parked beside the *Robin?*"

"That's true," Honey said. "She was a regular little mother to Sally, and she was the only one in the whole family who didn't look scared when the father ordered them inside the trailer."

"The eldest child in a big family," Trixie explained, "always grows up fast, because he or she has to help with the younger children. Why, when Brian was only nine Dad taught him how to shoot, but I'll bet he doesn't let Bobby, who's the baby, touch a gun until he's fifteen." She laughed. "I was the baby in our family until Bobby was born six years ago. And was I ever spoiled!"

"I don't believe it," Honey objected. They cut through the clearing and peeked inside the tent, but everything was exactly as they had left it the evening before. "Your father and mother are too smart to spoil anyone," Honey continued as they began the slow climb to the shrubby mound. "You don't know how lucky you are, Trixie, to have such wonderful parents and three brothers."

"Cheer up," Trixie said, "you may not be an only child for long. We'll see to it that your mother meets Jim somehow. She couldn't help liking him an awful lot."

Honey looked at her with sudden suspicion. "You seem awfully optimistic this morning, Trixie. The way you've been talking one would think we'd already found Jim and Joeanne, not to mention the red trailer." She sighed. "I don't think we're going to see anything from the top of that hill, and I'm sure we've lost Bud for good."

And then they heard the sound of joyful barking, and in another minute Bud came wriggling out from the underbrush. Honey scooped him into her arms and he licked her face happily, but he did not look at all as though he had spent a forlorn night in the woods. His coat was sleek and free of mud and burrs, and his tummy was the firm, rounded tummy of a puppy who has just bolted a large and satisfying breakfast.

"Well, that's that," Trixie cried, and pushing past Honey, raced to the top of the hill. At first she squinted to the east of the main highway and saw the Smith farm and the neat green rows of healthy plants in the rich brown earth of the truck garden. The abandoned orchard sloped away from the cleared land near the house, and, shading her eyes with one hand, Trixie caught a glimpse of the peaked roof of the old high-ceilinged barn down in the hollow.

So, she thought excitedly, *you can see it from here too.* Then she turned around and stared in the opposite direction, and what she saw made her scream at the top of her lungs to Honey. The rise of ground she was standing on, dropped down sharply on the west side to another hollow, and, parked in a small cleared space between tall evergreens, was the missing red trailer!

"Honey, Honey," she yelled. "We've found it at last." And as Honey hurried to join her she added breathlessly, "At least, Bud did. See, Sally's playing on the step. That's where your little black puppy spent the night."

Honey was too thrilled to do anything but stare for a minute. "You knew it all along," she got out finally in an accusing voice. "That's why you've been so cheerful all morning."

"I only guessed," Trixie told her. "If I'd been wrong, you would have died of disappointment. Come on! Let's go make a nice neighborly call on the Darnells."

Trixie was already slipping and sliding down the steep side of the hill, but Honey hung back. "They won't be at all glad to see us," she objected. "They'll be furious that we discovered their hiding place."

Trixie tripped on a stone and sat down suddenly, clutching at the branches of a scrub pine tree to keep from skidding all the way to the bottom. But the branches slipped through her fingers and, a second later, Trixie was sprawling on her back at the foot of the hill.

"Oh, oh," Honey cried, thinking Trixie must be hurt. And she stumbled headlong down to help her to her feet.

Both of Trixie's elbows were skinned but otherwise

she was all right, and she stood up, brushing the dirt from the seat of her dungarees. "That's one way of getting someplace quickly," she began with a rueful chuckle, and stopped with her mouth open as she saw Mrs. Darnell hurrying toward them under the cedar trees in the dense woods of the hollow.

"Oh, please go away," she sobbed when she came closer. "*Please!* Don't you think you've caused us enough trouble already?"

Trixie stared at her, tongue-tied, but Honey said quickly, "We haven't meant to cause you any trouble, Mrs. Darnell. We only—"

The woman covered her tired face with her thin, work-worn hands and burst into tears. "So you know our name now," she groaned. "Darney said you'd never give up until you tracked us down. I've been a fool. I thought you were kind. I even hoped Joeanne might be with you. She said you were nice girls, and we've never laid eyes on her since she took back your puppy. I've prayed every night since she ran away that she had hidden in your trailer and that she was safe in your care."

Impulsively, Honey put her arms around the woman's shaking shoulders. "Don't cry, Mrs. Darnell," she begged. "We are your friends, really and truly we are."

The frail woman pulled away from her. *"Friends!"* she repeated hoarsely. "You've been spying on us from the beginning and setting your dog on us. You knew how my little Sally loved him. You knew he would lead you to our hiding place. I should have shut him out last night and left him to shift for himself in the woods. He's been the cause of all our troubles."

"I'm terribly sorry," Honey cried, on the verge of tears herself now. "We never meant to spy on you. And we've been trying to find Joeanne ever since she ran away."

"It was your dog that made her do it," Mrs. Darnell sobbed. " 'It's bad enough to have a thief for a father,' she told me, my oldest girl, and my only comfort. 'But when my little sister starts taking after her father and stealing too, I can't bear it.' And those were the last words she spoke."

Trixie found her voice at last. "You mustn't worry about Joeanne any more, Mrs. Darnell," she got out. "She's perfectly safe and a friend of ours has been taking good care of her."

Mrs. Darnell stopped crying and hope gleamed in her reddened eyes. "Are you telling me the truth?" she demanded. "How can I trust you? Darney had a fine job with a good home for us at the Smith farm, and then you girls turned up. He was going to return the trailer to Mr. Lynch just as soon as the beans were picked, but when Sally told us she had seen you from the upstairs window, Darney wouldn't stay at the Smiths' another night. Oh, why did you have to ruin everything?"

She began to weep again but stopped abruptly as Trixie suddenly shouted. "Lynch! Oh, now I remember where I saw the *Robin* before. It belongs to Diana Lynch's father. They have a big place just outside of Sleepyside on the river," she explained to Honey in a rush of words. "Diana was in my class at school last year and invited me for lunch one Saturday. She showed me inside their trailer, but I'd forgotten all about it until this minute."

Mrs. Darnell wiped her eyes with a corner of her apron and set her thin shoulders. "There's no use pretending any more," she told Trixie. "Darney should never have done it, but what else could he do with four children and me so sick I could hardly move from room to room? The landlord said we'd have to get out the first of August if we didn't pay the rent. There were doctor bills and hospital bills and Darney barely on his feet again after the operation on his eye. And the farm not producing anything, what with him too sick to do the spring planting." She looked at them, imploring for

sympathy. "Then Mr. Lynch stopped by one morning and asked Darney to keep an eye on his house while he and his family were away on vacation. He was our nearest neighbor, you see, and very friendly although Darney was too proud to let him know about our troubles. So after the Lynches had gone, Darney went over to see if the house was locked up and everything as it should be, and there in the big garage was the trailer, all hitched up and ready to go with the keys in the tow car."

"The Lynches must have planned to take their vacation in the *Robin* and changed their minds at the last minute," Trixie put in.

Mrs. Darnell nodded in agreement. "The temptation was too much for Darney. He couldn't go off and look for work, leaving me, too weak to stand, with the care of the children. He knew he'd find work on one of the farms upstate—he knows this part of the country—his family once owned Wilson Ranch."

"And so," Honey finished sympathetically, "he just borrowed the *Robin,* planning to return it before the Lynches came home."

"That's right," Mrs. Darnell said. "But it was very wrong of us and we deserve to be punished. We've never drawn a happy breath since we started out. What with having to keep the children cooped up inside whenever we stopped for fear one of them would prattle and give away our secret. And then my big girl, my Joeanne—" She broke down again.

Trixie couldn't stand it another minute. "You haven't got a thing to worry about, Mrs. Darnell," she said firmly. "I know Mr. Lynch and he's just about the kindest man alive. He'll understand why you had to borrow his trailer. Why, he's got four or five children of his own, all younger than Diana. I'm going right back to Autoville and call him up and tell him the whole story. Just you wait and see. He'll tell the police to stop looking for the *Robin*. Then Mr. Darnell can leave you with the Smiths while he returns the trailer."

"It's too late for that," Mrs. Darnell wailed. "The Smiths will never take us back, and I think Darney has already been arrested, he's been gone so long. Oh, if only he'd been willing to let well enough alone, but no, he had to go and risk being caught himself to put the troopers on the trail of those thieves!"

Trixie and Honey gasped in unison. "Was it Mr. Darnell who called headquarters yesterday?" Trixie demanded in amazement. "Did he know that the Smiths' old barn was the trailer thieves' hide-out?"

Mrs. Darnell nodded tearfully. "Darney was out searching for some sign of Joeanne. He thought at first she might have gone to Wilson Ranch because she's heard him speak of his old home so often, and how as a boy he used to swim in a quarry. Then yesterday around noon he caught sight of the roof of an old barn down in the hollow on the other side of the road. He looked inside it, hoping she might be hiding there and saw this big van and valuable trailer equipment lying around. Then, not an hour later, he stumbled across the same van hitched to a trailer in the woods on this side of the road. Nothing would do but he must walk five miles to the nearest gas station and risk being arrested himself while he tips off the police."

She smiled through her tears, and Trixie saw that, in spite of her worries, Mrs. Darnell was proud of her husband. "That's Darney for you," she said, "and Joeanne is exactly like him. They have the same thick black hair that grows like weeds, and they're both as stubborn as mules and as honest as the day is long. If it hadn't been for my being so sickly, my Darney would never have touched that trailer."

A twig crackled in the woods and all three of them jumped as a tall, broad-shouldered trooper stepped out from behind the thick trunk of an old oak tree.

Chapter 17
Mrs. Smith Takes Over

Out of the corner of her eye, Trixie saw with inner amusement that gentle, kindhearted Honey had doubled up her fists and looked prepared to scratch the trooper's eyes out. Trixie herself let out a long, pent-up sigh of relief, for the trooper with the sergeant's stripes on his sleeves was standing there uncertainly, as though torn between his sense of duty and sympathy for Mrs. Darnell.

"I'm sorry to have been eavesdropping, ma'am," he told her in a most apologetic voice. "I saw that blond kid sleigh-riding down the hill on the seat of her pants and came over to investigate." His kind blue eyes twinkled. "So it was your husband who called headquarters yesterday?"

Mrs. Darnell's lower lip trembled and she caught it between her teeth. "Yes, it was," she said defiantly, "and it was he who took the red trailer you've been looking high and low for these past few days." She pointed through the trees. "There it is, waiting for you, and it'll be the answer to my prayers if you take it away."

"Now then, take it easy, ma'am," the sergeant said soothingly. "Our orders about that red trailer have been changed since yesterday. When we notified Mr. Lynch that it hadn't been stolen by one of the gang that's been operating in this neck of the woods, he said for us to skip it. Said he'd just learned that one of his very good neighbors had borrowed it and that he would be very much obliged if we would have this fact announced on the radio as soon as possible."

The sergeant twirled his cap. "Couldn't help over-hearing what you were telling these girls just now, Mrs. Darnell. Sounds as though you were the neighbors Mr. Lynch told us about on the phone. Guess Mr. Lynch only just heard about the trouble you people have been hav-ing. I figured you might like to have a motorcycle escort down the river when your husband drives the *Robin* back to Sleepyside. You can't always tell how the cops in some of those small towns might act if they saw a red trailer passing through. Might get all excited and ask you a lot of foolish questions."

Mrs. Darnell's thin face turned pale, then red and then pale again. "Oh, officer," she gasped, "we don't deserve such kindness."

The trooper went on as though he hadn't heard her. "And then there's the question of the rewards. All together they mount up to quite a tidy sum, and we boys would like to add a little something to it. I don't even have to ask the men in my troop." He reached into his hip pocket and produced a thick leather wallet. "In the first place," he said, "the disappearance of the *Robin* fixed those trailer thieves. As long as it didn't show up right away the way the other ones did, the reporters in the press and on the air kept howling for action. All the hue and cry ruined the crooks' racket. Smart of your husband to figure that out, Mrs. Darnell. And very modest of him not to give us his name when he tipped us off. We could use a man like that." He slipped a twenty-dollar bill into the pocket of her apron. "Just a small token of our appreciation for all the time and trouble you saved us. If Mr. Darnell ever wants a job, let me know."

It was all Trixie could do to keep from throwing her arms around the trooper's neck and hugging him. He slapped his cap back on his head and saluted smartly. "I'll be getting back to headquarters now. When Mr. Darnell is ready for the motorcycle escort, have him drop by and just say the word."

His broad shoulders disappeared through the trees before anyone could utter a sound.

And then the silence was broken by Mrs. Darnell's weeping, but this time she was crying for joy. "That dear, kind man," she sobbed. "We don't deserve any of it, but I'll pray for his health and happiness every night of my life. If we could only find Joeanne now, our troubles would be over."

Trixie reached out and patted her hand. "I know where Joeanne is," she said with more confidence than she felt. "You go back and wait in the trailer for your husband. Honey and I will bring Joeanne to you."

Mrs. Darnell smiled shyly. "I believe you do know where my daughter is. I'm glad I was right about you girls. Deep down inside me I was sure from the beginning that I could trust you." She turned and darted away like a timid little gray squirrel.

"Trixie Belden," Honey said sternly, "I'm ashamed of you. You had no business arousing false hope in that poor woman. You don't know where Joeanne is any more than I do."

Trixie tugged at Honey's bare arm. "I don't *know* but I'm practically certain. Both Jim and Joeanne are not far away. Come on!"

Bud sat down on his haunches mournfully, as though undecided as to whether he should follow Mrs. Darnell or his mistress. Honey bit her lip. "I love that little black nuisance," she said more to herself than to Trixie, "but I think he'd be happier with a family of children than with me all alone in that big old house. Wait," she told Trixie. "I won't be a minute, but I want to give him to Sally right now and get it over and done with."

Trixie watched Honey disappear through the trees with Bud frolicking at her heels. "Honey's mother has just got to adopt Jim," she said grimly through her teeth. "He'll be a perfect brother for Honey. Mrs. Wheeler has got to see it that way. *She's just got to!*"

Honey came running back then, her cheeks flushed and her hazel eyes sparkling. "That Sally!" She panted as she followed Trixie around the base of the hill. "Her mother made her thank me, of course, but she was as fresh as paint about it. 'Thank you for bringing back my puppy,' she said like a little queen. 'He was losted but I won't let him get losted any more.' "

Trixie chuckled. "Sally makes me homesick for Bobby. He's an awful pest, but I guess I miss him even more than I do Brian and Mart. Oh, Honey," she went on enthusiastically, "won't it be wonderful to be back home again? We can ride every day and go swimming in your lake, and—"

"Nothing will ever be the same again without Jim," Honey interrupted sadly. "Please don't keep me in the dark any more. What makes you think we're going to find him and Joeanne close by?"

"I don't know why we were both so dumb we didn't guess before," Trixie admitted. "Remember what Mrs. Smith said about two boys who bicycled up to the farmhouse and offered to help pick the beans?"

Honey nodded. "I don't see what that's got to do with it. I thought for a while that her hired hand who fell out of the old apple tree might have been Jim, but Jim is much too smart to have done anything so stupid."

The neglected path they had been following came out abruptly on the main highway about twenty yards south of the entrance to the Smith farm.

"That hired hand wasn't Jim," Trixie said, "but the big brother Mrs. Smith said was so husky and knew his way around a farm, *is.* Why, Honey, she even called the little brother, Joe. I didn't put two and two together until Mrs. Darnell was talking about how much Joeanne is like her father. She said both of them have hair that grows like weeds, and I thought to myself, 'Now both of them have haircuts too.' And right at that moment I got a mental picture of Joeanne in those patched blue jeans without her pigtails. And I saw at once that anybody would take her for a thin little boy."

Honey covered her face with her hands. "Oh, Trixie," she moaned, "we *were* dumb. Do you think it's too late? Do you think Jim may already have left the Smiths?"

"Not Jim," Trixie said firmly. "He'd never leave until

the bean crop is in. They couldn't even go down in the garden yesterday after the rain for fear of spreading rust through the beans, but now that the sun has dried off everything, you can be sure that Jim is down there right now, picking away like mad."

Honey began to laugh, rather hysterically, Trixie thought. "I can't stand it, I can't stand it," she cried, grabbing Trixie's hand and starting to run. "To think we were sitting in Mrs. Smith's kitchen yesterday eating chocolate layer cake and drinking spiced grape juice while Jim was only half an acre away!"

"Jim *and* Joeanne," Trixie agreed breathlessly as Honey dragged her into the Smith driveway. "I was only half listening to Mrs. Smith when she went on and on about the two boys. I was thinking about the abandoned barn and how it must be down in the hollow below the old orchard. The sky was clouding over and I wanted to get away so we could explore before it poured."

"If we'd only waited a few more minutes," Honey gasped. "Jim and Joeanne would have come up from the garden at the first drop of rain."

"That's right," Trixie said, forcing Honey to slow down to a walk. "Let's get our breath before we barge into the house. Mrs. Smith will think we're crazy." She mopped her face with her handkerchief and Honey followed suit.

It was terribly hot and sultry and the sun was shining through a haze that hung over the fields below the farmhouse.

"It can't be later than ten o'clock," Honey said thoughtfully. "Maybe it's still too wet to pick beans. Maybe they're—"

And then they saw them—Jim and Joeanne, strolling among the gnarled apple trees in the old orchard. Perched on Jim's shoulder, just as though he belonged there, was Jimmy Crow, looking as smug as if he had solved all the mysteries himself.

Honey stood stock still, too thrilled to move for a minute, and even Trixie could only get out a weak yell. "Jim," she called, and then more loudly, "Jim! It's Honey and Trixie."

Joeanne, looking for all the world like a miniature copy of her father before Mrs. Smith had closely cropped his hair, grabbed Jim's hand and edged closer to him.

"It's those girls," Trixie heard her murmur. "The ones I told you about. Sally stole their puppy, but she didn't mean any harm; she just doesn't understand."

But Jim wasn't listening. A broad grin spread over his freckled face. "Well, I never!" he shouted. "You two tracked me down in less than a week, you sleuths, you!"

Honey seized one of his strong brown hands and

shook it while Trixie clutched Jim's arm excitedly. She felt like laughing and crying at the same time, and now that they had found him, she couldn't think of a word to say.

Jimmy Crow broke the silence with a loud, hoarse "Caw" of disgust and flew away, flapping his wings, to the top of a tall maple tree. He glared down at them jealously as Trixie and Honey and Jim all began talking at once.

It was bedlam.

"It sure is good to see you girls again—"

"Oh, Jim, my father went to school with your father—"

"You don't have to worry about Jonesy any more, Jim, because Mr. Rainsford—"

And then Joeanne chimed in, making the confusion even worse.

"I saw you riding down a road on horseback and hid in the woods—"

At last Jim held up his hand for silence. "One at a time, puh-leeze," he commanded. "And is there any reason why we can't have a second breakfast in Mrs. Smith's nice sunny kitchen while we talk?"

"Wonderful," Trixie cried. "She's such a darling I know she'll love hearing every word we say."

In a few minutes Mrs. Smith was scrambling eggs, to which she added chunks of yellow cheese. As usual, she dominated the conversation.

"Now mind you," she admonished Honey who hadn't had a chance to utter a complete sentence since all four of them had gathered around the big kitchen table. "Nobody told me in so many words that Joeanne was a boy, nor did anyone come right out and tell me that they were brothers." She poured a cup of cream into the mixture and stirred vigorously. "I thought it was simpler to jump to conclusions, and ask no questions, with help as hard to get as it is. Now Nat, only last night, said to me, 'Mary,' he said, 'they are no more brothers than you and I are. Brother and *sister*, maybe, but they resemble each other about as much as that pet crow of yours resembles a peacock.'

" 'My pet crow, indeed,' I said, changing the subject because I knew as well as Nat did that the little one here was a girl and that somebody had done a clumsy job of hacking off her hair." Her black eyes twinkled at Jim. "I'll give you a few lessons in barbering before you go, boy. You're handy around a farm, I won't deny, but you'd never get a job in a beauty parlor." She ran one hand through Joeanne's thick, roughly cropped hair. "Reminds me of the mess Mr. Darnell's mane was until I took shears and razor to him!"

Joeanne gulped and started to say something but Jim broke in sheepishly, "Ah, I didn't want to hack off her pigtails, Mrs. Smith, and we didn't plan to fool you—not that we did. When I found the poor kid crying in the woods not far from my camp, half of her hair was tangled in a bramble bush and she couldn't get loose. I *had* to chop her free."

Joeanne nodded. "And then I looked so funny with only one braid and I'd lost both hair ribbons by then, so I made him chop off the other pigtail." She smiled across the table at Trixie and Honey. "If I hadn't hurried into the thicket to hide from you, my hair wouldn't have got snarled in the brambles. I was afraid you'd take me to an orphan asylum, and I wanted to find Daddy and Mommy." Tears welled up in her big black eyes. "It was awful of me to run away and leave Mommy with the babies to take care of, but when Sally took your puppy I couldn't stand it any longer." She folded her arms on the table and buried her face in the crook of one elbow. "Daddy's not a thief, I tell you. He's *not!*"

"There, there," Mrs. Smith said, gathering the thin little shoulders into her arms. "Nobody said he was, lambie, and you mustn't worry any more. Everything will turn out all right, just wait and see."

She glared defiantly at Jim, who hadn't the vaguest idea of what she was talking about. "Do you take

Nathaniel Smith for a fool?" she demanded belligerently. "I'm the one who takes in every stray tramp, dog, boy, girl, and crow that taps at my door and I ask no questions. Although I must say for myself I do know a man's daughter when I see her, especially when she's the spit and image of her old man as this one is."

Jim's green eyes popped. "Are you telling me, Mrs. Smith, that you know Joeanne's father?"

"Know him?" Mrs. Smith roared. "Didn't I feed him three helpings of kidney stew only night before last in this very kitchen? And Nat insisting that I had nourished a viper until I made him walk to the gas station and telephone this very morning and check with the police on the license plates of that borrowed trailer. 'Stolen,' says Nat; 'Borrowed,' says I. So I sent him right back to the gas station to call Mr. Lynch himself. And what does he tell Nat? 'The Darnells?' he asks. 'Why, they're my very good neighbors. Please tell them they're welcome to the use of the *Robin* for as long as they like.' "

She chuckled triumphantly. "I would have called the man myself if our phone wasn't as dead as a doornail since the heavy rain yesterday."

Joeanne raised her face and her eyes were starry now. "Then my father didn't steal that trailer, Mrs. Smith? He only borrowed it just as Mommy said?"

"Of course, lamb," Mrs. Smith assured her. "And even if he had stolen it, you had no business running away. If you were mine, I'd take the back of a hairbrush to you, and I may yet, but not until there's more meat on your bones."

It was so obvious that Mrs. Smith was probably incapable of even swatting a fly that everyone seated around the table burst into laughter.

When Jim sobered, he said, "So your phone was out of order. Every time I got a chance I've been trying to call police headquarters, but I thought that buzzing sound meant somebody was on the line."

"And what were you going to call the police about?" Mrs. Smith demanded as she heaped the egg and cheese mixture on plates and filled four tall glasses with thick, creamy milk.

Jim looked embarrassed, and Honey broke in quickly, "I knew you'd do it, Jim, or at least try to. After you let the air out of the tire and hid the jack—"

"It doesn't matter now, anyway," Trixie interrupted. "Joeanne's father notified the police, Jim, and we were hiding in the old barn when the troopers arrested Jeff and Al."

Jim stopped with his fork halfway to his mouth. "You girls certainly get around." He grinned. "I suppose the whereabouts of Joeanne's family at the moment is no mystery to you, either."

"It isn't," Trixie told him tartly. "And as soon as we've finished eating Mrs. Smith out of house and home, we're going to take Joeanne there, all three of us."

"Not me," Jim said. "I've got beans to pick and then I'm off again. I plan to hit the road tonight."

"You'll do nothing of the sort," Mrs. Smith boomed at the top of her lungs. "The very idea! Going away just when I've grown to love you like one of my seven sons." She patted her album locket. "Nat's baby picture will have to come out, and I'll put one of you in its place, Jim Frayne."

Jim's face turned white and the freckles stood out on the bridge of his nose. "Then—you—know—who I am?" he muttered under his breath.

"And why not?" Mrs. Smith sank down in her rocker. "I may be fat but I can still read the newspapers, and if I remember correctly there was a story on the front page about a missing heir just a week ago today. The nephew of one James Winthrop Frayne of Sleepyside, I recall. It is none of my business why you want to run away from half a million dollars, but when you knocked on my back door asking for work and I ask you your name, and you say, 'Call me Win,' and I say,

'Short for Winthrop?' and you nod that red head of yours, what else can I think but that you didn't get burned alive in that fire?"

She stopped for breath and Honey said, "It's all right, Jim. You haven't anything to worry about."

He acted as though he hadn't heard her. "Half a million dollars," he repeated dazedly. "Then Trixie was right." His mouth widened into a smile. "Why, I can even buy my freedom from Jonesy with that much money. I'll take enough to see me through college and he can have the rest."

"Indeed, he can't," Trixie broke in. "He won't see one cent of it. Mr. Rainsford, who's the executor of your great-uncle's estate, has already made arrangements to appoint another guardian." It was on the tip of her tongue to tell him that Honey hoped her parents would adopt him, but before she could begin, heavy feet clumped up the steps to the door.

On the other side of the screen was the tallest and thinnest man Trixie had ever seen. "Well, I found him, Mary," Farmer Nathaniel Smith said as he walked into the kitchen. Right behind him was Joeanne's father. He looked so different with his closely cropped hair that Trixie would never have recognized him if Joeanne hadn't screamed, "Daddy!"

Chapter 18
Jim's Decision

Joeanne jumped out of her chair, knocking it over and spilling her milk at the same time. Mr. Darnell, his face wreathed in smiles, pushed by Farmer Smith and gathered his daughter into his arms.

"It took you long enough," Mrs. Smith told her husband, trying hard to keep back the tears as she watched Joeanne clinging to her father.

The tall, thin man folded himself tiredly into a straight-back chair. "Tramped every inch of the woods on both sides of the road," he said in a monotone. "Found the camp where Win here was hiding out before he came to work for us. You were right about him too, Mary. Saw his name on a christening mug under the blanket on his bunk."

Mrs. Smith rocked back and forth placidly. "We've been married thirty years," she told Honey and Trixie, "and yet it never fails to surprise Nat when I'm right. Go on, lamb," she urged her husband. "Where did you finally find the Darnells?"

"I followed the stream by Win's camp," Mr. Smith

continued, "and then I heard a dog barking. Sounded as though it came from Frog Hollow and sure enough, it did. In a few minutes more I saw the *Robin* in a clearing and Mr. Darnell himself in the tow car, ready to drive away." He sighed. "If I'd been delayed sixty seconds I would have lost the best man I ever hired."

"No, you wouldn't," Mr. Darnell said quietly, still holding Joeanne close to him. "I was on my way over here to ask you if you'd take me back after I'd returned Mr. Lynch's trailer."

"Oh, Daddy," Joeanne cried, "are we going to live with the Smiths? Please, Daddy, I'd rather live here than anywhere else in the world."

Mrs. Smith dabbed at her eyes with the corner of her apron. "I declare," she said to her husband. "The Lord is certainly looking out for us. Here I was counting on three children to fill up those empty bedrooms and now we're going to have five. Jim Frayne's going to stay on too, Nat. You tell him he has to, although what use he'll have here for half a million dollars is more than I can say." She turned on Jim, scolding to disguise her fear that he might not stay. "If you must go to college, I suppose you must, but you'll earn your bed and board vacation-time, I can tell you. There'll be no lying abed in this house, even on Christmas Day, what with snow to be shoveled and logs to be cut and corn to be popped for four little hungry children."

Jim's green eyes were misty as he grinned at Mrs. Smith. "I'll be here my very first Christmas vacation," he promised, "and Thanksgiving too, if you'll have me."

At that Honey burst into tears. "I want him for my brother," she wailed unashamedly. "You don't need him, Mrs. Smith, not with all the Darnells. But I haven't anybody."

Mr. Smith came to the rescue. "There, there," he said soothingly. "Pay no attention to Mary. She's never satisfied no matter how many blessings the good Lord bestows on her. Seven sons of her own she has, and five grandsons. I must say I'd like to have young Frayne stay with us, but if you have other plans for him, so be it."

Trixie could not help laughing at the way people were calmly arranging Jim's life for him. He winked at her and stood up. "It's dry enough now to work in the garden. Let's all go pick beans."

"We'll do nothing of the kind." Mrs. Smith bristled. "If Mr. Darnell will kindly go and get the rest of his family I'll try to scrape up enough food for a party. We'll have a celebration this very afternoon, beans or no beans. I never cared for them anyway, nasty tasteless things unless drowned in fresh butter."

"Get to your baking, Mary," Mr. Smith said mildly. "I can finish the beans myself. Win—I mean, Jim—did so much yesterday morning there's hardly a bushel left on the vines."

"I'd like to finish the job, sir," Jim said, but Mr. Smith waved him away.

"These girls," he said in his flat, expressionless voice, "would like to have you to themselves, I think, for a little while anyway. Come back for tea, all of you, but right now let's clear out the kitchen. Mary likes to be alone when she bakes."

Mrs. Smith was already yanking pie tins out of a corner cupboard, and did not seem to notice when the others filed out the back door.

Mr. Smith headed for the garden, and Mr. Darnell and Joeanne started down the driveway toward the macadam road. Trixie grabbed Jim's hand.

"Come on," she cried, "we'll cut through the orchard and the fields to Autoville. I can't wait to show you to Miss Trask and telephone Mr. Rainsford that we found you."

"I still can't believe it." Honey sighed as she hurried along on the other side of Jim. "Now, if only Mother—"

"Sh-h," Trixie stopped her. "Let's not talk about that now. I want to hear what Jim's been doing since he left the mansion."

"Well, there isn't much to tell," Jim said. "I bought a bike and headed for this part of the country. Rigged up a camp in the woods and tried to get a job at one of those boys' camps I told you about. But no luck. I found Joeanne caught by her hair to a bramble bush and turned my camp over to her while I moved to the old barn down there in the hollow." He grinned. "You seem to know more about those trailer thieves than I do, although how you knew I loosened the core valve on their tire is more than I can guess."

Trixie explained and when she had finished Jim chuckled. "If I'd only known Mr. Darnell was on their trail too, I wouldn't have worried so. But, as a matter of fact, I was pretty sure the troopers would find that van while it was still hitched up to the stolen trailer. Then all they had to do was wait there calmly until Al and Jeff came back with the jack. That's why I just tossed it into an empty stall instead of taking it away with me. I wanted them to go back to the van and get caught, you see?"

"In between fixing that tire and hiding the jack," Honey said thoughtfully, "you must have been picking beans in the Smiths' garden."

"That's right," Jim said. "Early yesterday morning I got Joeanne and we biked to the farmhouse. I'd bought her a secondhand bike the day before in the village. We

255

didn't really stop at the Smiths' to get a job, but to try to find out if Joeanne's father had tried to get work there. It seemed logical, you know, that he would want to settle down in the same part of the country where he spent his boyhood. Say," he interrupted himself suddenly, "Wilson Ranch is a swell place. I'd sure like to get a job there."

"You can, now," Honey said in a sad little voice. "But, oh, Jim, I do wish you'd spend the rest of the summer with us."

"Now, Honey," Trixie cried impatiently. "Don't start that again. Wait until Jim meets your family."

Jim chuckled. "If they're half as nice as you, Honey, I'll be satisfied. What were you saying about our fathers going to school together?"

"They did," Honey said. "Mr. Rainsford told me so. He wants to appoint Dad as your guardian, you see."

"That would be swell," Jim said enthusiastically. "But maybe when your dad gets a look at me, he won't want the bother of it."

They hurried around the Autoville park and stopped at the *Swan* door. Pinned to it was a note from Miss Trask: *Come right over to the cafeteria.*

"It can't be lunchtime yet," Honey wondered out loud. "Why does she want us over there?"

Trixie shrugged. "Let's go. We can telephone Mr. Rainsford from there."

But Mr. Rainsford himself was waiting for them in the lounge, and even more surprising was the sight of Honey's father and mother who, with Miss Trask and the lawyer, were gathered around a large table in one corner of the room.

"Mother," Honey gasped and ran across the room to throw her arms around her parents and kiss them both. Later she told Trixie that she had never acted so impulsively before, but in her anxiety about Jim she momentarily forgot her shyness. It was the best thing she had ever done, for Mrs. Wheeler forgot her own shyness and hugged Honey, frankly weeping.

"My precious baby," she crooned, smoothing Honey's hair with one slim, restless hand. "I've missed you so, and Dad did too, so we decided to charter a plane and fly down this morning."

Trixie thought Honey's mother was the most beautiful woman she had ever seen, and she looked just the way Honey would look in another twenty years. She was tall and slender with wavy light-brown hair, and she turned her enormous hazel eyes to Trixie and said, holding out her free hand, "You're Trixie, I know. Honey has written me so much about you. And is this Jim?"

Jim smiled and shook hands with Honey's parents. Then he was introduced to Miss Trask and Mr. Rainsford.

Mr. Wheeler said with a wide grin, "I'd have known you anywhere, Jim. You look exactly as your dad did when I last saw him."

Honey's mother smiled up at her husband. "He doesn't look unlike you, Matthew," she said and added to Jim, "Come sit beside me, please. I suppose you know Honey thinks you're just about the most wonderful person on this earth?"

Jim flushed and turned to Mr. Rainsford. "It was nice of you, sir, to come all the way up here from New York to meet me."

"How did that happen?" Trixie demanded. "You didn't know we'd found him, Mr. Rainsford."

The lawyer's eyes twinkled. "No, but something had to be done about him at once. I'm going to South America on Saturday and I'll be gone several months. I decided that if you girls hadn't found Jim by now, I'd have to notify the police."

"I'm sorry I caused you so much trouble, sir," Jim said, finally sitting down beside Honey and her mother. "I didn't know, and my stepfather—"

"Don't give *him* a second thought," Mr. Rainsford

said. He turned to Honey's father. "Well, Wheeler, what do you think? Do you want to take over my charge while I'm gone? We don't have to make any permanent arrangements until after you two have tried it out. I think Jim deserves a good home, and I can't think of a better person to look after his inheritance."

Mr. Wheeler laughed. "I'll take good care of his money, but as to having me as his guardian, why I think that's up to Jim."

Jim looked uncomfortable, and Mrs. Wheeler touched his hand lightly with her long, tapering fingers. "You don't have to answer now, Jim," she said quietly. "We'd like to take out adoption papers right away, but it wouldn't be fair not to give you a chance to get to know us better first."

Jim grinned, his embarrassment gone. "It isn't that, Mrs. Wheeler," he said sincerely. "I know Honey and there isn't anyone I'd rather have for a sister. But you and Mr. Wheeler don't know anything about *me.*"

"We know more than you think," Mrs. Wheeler said quickly.

Trixie couldn't keep silent another minute. "He's just great, Mrs. Wheeler," she exploded, and then she told them all about how Jim had taken care of Joeanne and had fixed the tire on the trailer thieves' van, and how

Mrs. Smith wanted him to stay with her forever and ever.

"If you don't adopt him, *she* will," Trixie finished breathlessly while Jim, who had tried to interrupt her several times, sighed aloud with relief.

"Oh, heck," he groaned, "Trixie's trying to make me out a hero. Don't pay any attention to her!"

Honey reached over and tapped her father's knee to get his attention. "Please, Daddy," she begged. "Adopt Jim right this minute. You don't know Mrs. Smith. She's the smartest woman I ever heard of. If you don't watch out, she'll get him first."

Jim burst into laughter. "Mrs. Smith will have her hands full with that Darnell family." He sobered suddenly and said to Mr. Wheeler, "I don't know how you feel about it, sir, but as far as I'm concerned I'd consider myself very lucky if *you'd* consider trying me out for the rest of the summer."

"Consider!" Mr. Wheeler's sandy eyebrows shot up. "We've been trying to tell you for the past half hour that we would consider *our*selves lucky if you'd consider having us."

Mrs. Wheeler broke in with a tinkling little laugh. "Oh, Matthew," she giggled, "you and all your *consider*s. For heaven's sake, tell the boy and Mr. Rainsford that they can consider the matter settled."

"Now, you're doing it, Mother." Honey smiled. "Oh, Jim, it *is* settled, isn't it?"

Jim's green eyes sparkled, and a slow grin spread over his freckled face. "From where I sit, it is, Sis, so you'd better watch your step from now on."

Trixie knew she was going to burst into tears of joy any minute, so she jumped up and ran out.

She turned as a husky voice behind her said, "They're waiting for you at a table inside." Jim gave her a little push. "In you go, kid; I'm top man around here now."

Trixie tossed her head, grinning. "Just wait till Brian and Mart come back from camp, Jim Frayne. Then we'll see who's boss around here."

But she followed Jim meekly through the door, already planning the fun they would have during the warm September days before school opened. She and Honey would learn to shoot so they could go hunting with the boys in the fall and in the winter there would be sledding down the steep hill from the Wheeler house and skating on the lake.

"Sometimes," she decided, "dreams *do* come true."